EDENS GARDEN

THE NIA RIVERS ADVENTURES BOOK 5

INES JOHNSON

THOSE JOHNSON GIRLS

Copyright © 2018, 2020, Ines Johnson. All rights reserved. This novel is a work of fiction. All characters, places, and incidents described in this publication are used fictitiously, or are entirely fictional. No part of this publication may be reproduced or transmitted, in any form or by any means, except by an authorized retailer, or with written permission of the author.

Cover by Dark Queen Designs

Manufactured in the United States of America
First Edition March 2018
Second Edition October 2020

CHAPTER ONE

*E*very story has an ending. No matter how long or twisting or winding, or if you go in reverse, or up or down, or if you cross over your previous path a couple of times and then circle back around again, the end of the line is still inevitable.

Circles aren't immune. The curved paths still abide the properties of existence. They have a starting point and a stopping one. Though it might be harder to decipher the beginning and end, those points are still there. There is still a boundary line that's inescapable.

Every life is a line. There is a set point that enters the planet, strikes the pavement, or marks the parchment. And there is a terminal point where all traces of the individual, the impression, the imprint cease.

All things come to an end. And that included my life. I was immortal, but I had never truly believed I'd live forever. The math wasn't on my side.

Here's my point: if this was the end, why hadn't I ceased to be?

Thoughts zigged and zagged in my mind. The shape of my mind wasn't closed like a circle. It felt boundless, open. There were no lines, no corners, no curves. All of this would've perplexed my friend Euclid, who was credited with having systematized the mathematical concepts of geometry.

The wiry old man with a long, white beard in two parallel lines that draped from his chin was fond of saying that *a line is length without breadth.* I remembered the day he'd said it. The Alexandrian sun kissed my skin as I sat on the white stone steps outside the Library of Alexandria.

My memories of five hundred years ago weren't this vivid. This particular memory was more than two millennia old, but it was clear and detailed, from the spice of the eucalyptus trees and the spice of cardamom. And those weren't the only things I remembered.

I remembered, well, everything. Was this death?

Swimming in the mire of the crystal-clear memories of my life?

Three thousand years of memories swirled around in my head like a galaxy. Each specific memory was a starry point of light. I only had to reach out and touch. I reached for one of the farthest ones.

In the memory that I caught hold of, I was bent over a slab of clay. Men and women surrounded me as I etched wedged shapes on the tablet with a blunt reed. The shapes were pictures. More like pictograms. More exactly like cuneiform.

Oh? Would you look at that? I'd taught humanity one of its earliest forms of the written language.

I reached for another bright point in my memory, further back. This time I had a spade in my hand. I was digging. No surprise there. What surprised me was what I found in the dirt.

It was a giant skull with huge, vacant eye sockets, a long snout, and pointed teeth that were each the size of a man's hand. The people around me shouted and shrieked about giants, ogres, griffins, monsters. But I knew better.

I knew exactly what the bone was and what animal it belonged to. I'd seen this great reptile before, walking over the earth, flying through the sky, breathing light so bright it singed the treetops. But at that moment, I hadn't been able to remember the name of the magnificent creature. I knew it now: dragon.

I cleaned the dirt off the dragon's skull carefully, still unable to call it by its name in that time. Wrapping it up, I brought it back to the light to inspect it. I wracked my brain for all the information I had inside but couldn't come up with an answer. Instead of upsetting me, it thrilled me to know there were things that I didn't know.

I reached beyond that bright point of light and captured another memory. This one warmed my heart. The first time my heart had skipped a beat. See, there was a boy.

A boy with dark hair and soulful eyes. He was recreating life on parchment. He painted in wondrous color with such detail, it was hard to believe the rendition wasn't the real thing.

I marveled at his work. When he turned to me, the look on his face took my breath away. With just a glance, the connection was instant, complete, absolute, as if he'd touched me with his gaze. A light within him had shone on me, through me, and enveloped me. I knew in the bottom of my very being, of whatever I was, that the connection would be forever.

Only one other bright spot remained before that soul-altering one, and I reached for it. It was my first memory. My starting point, the moment I came into existence.

I remembered being swaddled, but not by cloth. By something soft and warm and spongy. It was red and pulsing. I couldn't move much, but didn't feel the need to.

I was safe. I was protected. I was loved. But then one day, that world turned me upside down. It pushed me out.

I was remembering my birth.

Red gave way to darkness and then a light so blinding that I cried out. A face peered down at me. The expression was inscrutable. Even as an infant at the start of this new life, I knew to be quiet while held in this enigmatic person's gaze.

My cry broke, abruptly as a pencil scratching off the end of a paper. The face didn't change in expression, but my silence felt like the right thing. The shimmer of approval pleased me. And then the face was gone.

Arms reached down and pulled me onto warm skin. That skin was toasty-brown and warm. Her face was clearly readable. Pink lips stretched wide, and my heart kicked into gear. I sighed as she cradled me next to a heart that matched the beating of mine.

The moment was perfect. I thought it would go on forever. It did not.

I'm certain it was a long moment, many years, decades even. But after some time, those arms fell away from my mature body. My mother had come to the end of her line, the acquittal of her imprint, the absolution of her impression, the annulment of her self as an individual.

My mother.

I'd had a mother. But she was gone. And now, so was I.

My eyes blinked open. Just as with my birth, a bright light blinded me. I squinted, but the light wasn't so harsh that it harmed me. Instead, it overwhelmed me.

It took a moment to get used to the glare, and then a face appeared. It wasn't my mother's face. It was the inscrutable face, the enigmatic face, the first face I ever remember seeing after leaving my mother's womb.

That face stared at me again. I gasped, sucking in air, but I didn't cry out. Still, somehow, I instinctively knew that any type of histrionics would not be appreciated, that it would displease this being. And I didn't want her displeasure.

Her. Yes, this being was female.

Her features were soft and rounded like a woman's. But *woman* seemed the wrong word. Female, feminine, those were right. Because I knew that, though female, she was not human.

She stood nude, peering down at me. Her body approximated female humanity, but there were things missing. Like breasts, for one.

She had a chest with bumps that could barely pass for an A cup. There were no nipples. Her hips were rounded and her abdomen flat. She had no belly button. Her limbs were long and toned. There were no muscles, but something told me she was stronger than she looked.

Her eyes were wide, abnormally so, but perfectly symmetrical. They covered a third of her face in a half moon-shaped crescent with no eyelids or lashes. She didn't blink, she only stared. It was a blinding, pupil-less stare with eyes the color of the sun that radiated the same heat.

There was no hair atop her head. Instead, there were raised nodes in a swirling pattern, much like the meditating Buddha statues decorating the temple of Angkor Wat in Cambodia.

I lay there in the pool of light as we stared at each other. She studied me, like a specimen in a lab. I tried to move, but my limbs wouldn't budge. Something invisible held me down to the lab table.

"Hold still," the female said, "or this will hurt."

She held up the index finger of one hand. Using the other hand, she peeled the skin from her finger. Just like in the kid's movie of an alien trying to phone home, her finger lit up. I couldn't hold my tongue any longer. I tore open my lips and screamed.

CHAPTER TWO

That finger came closer and closer to me.

Like a pinlight an optician uses to detect problems with your pupil. The bright light was worse than being plunged into darkness. I could see everything that was happening to me.

I was trapped in some type of lab, being dissected by some type of androgynous mad scientist. Only, she wasn't slicing through my body. When I looked down the table, I didn't see my body.

There was nothing there. I was a disembodied head. That's why I couldn't move.

If I hadn't been freaking out before, I sure as hell was now. Was this hell?

"Keep still, or I'll get your breasts crooked," she said. "I doubt he'd like that."

He? He who? And what did she mean she'd get my breasts crooked? I didn't have any breasts anymore. And that's when I felt my nipple tighten.

I looked down again. And there was my right boob. That glowing, alien finger hovered over my skin, not touching it. Actually, both of her hands moved over me. Her fingers moved like the two sides of a waltz, right and left coming together and then moving apart. Weaving in and out and around like knitting.

Yes. That's what she was doing. She was knitting skin around me. The me that I could see was a body of pure white light.

"I'm not dead," I said.

She said nothing. Her face was pinched in concentration as she worked on my abs. I figured I shouldn't interrupt her or my flat belly might turn into an eight-pack.

I wanted to say more, to ask a question, but I knew better. Well, I may have *known* better, but I didn't *do* better.

"I'm not dead," I repeated. "But I'm not exactly alive either."

She cocked her head to one side as though to examine me from another angle. In the space I was in, there was only that blinding light on every side, and even from the ceiling to the floor.

She waited for me to answer my own question. This was a test, the final exam of life. Unfortunately, I hadn't studied. Still, somehow, I knew the answer.

"I'm being reborn," I said.

The second it took for her to respond felt like an eternity stretched over infinity. Finally, she smiled. The skin forming on my back crawled. My toes tingled. My toes weren't completely covered by skin.

I reached up to my head, and my hand passed through the space where my head should be. I held up my hand. My fingers weren't the toasty brown they had been my entire life. They were the color of light. I was light. My light was slowly being encased inside skin. Flesh knitted over the light of my being, encasing me in the brown skin I'd originally been born with.

I looked back to the female. This time I asked a question. It was the most important question of my life. My old life and this new one.

"What am I?"

"What do you call yourself in this time?" the female asked.

I hated that she avoided my question, but her dodge felt familiar. I tried to move again, but I didn't understand how to move when I didn't quite have a body. I felt insubstantial as a being of pure light, like I could float away at any moment, or scatter and dissipate like a wave pulling back into a vast ocean. It was terrifying.

Even with my eyes shut, all was light.

I knew how to do this, but thinking about it was too much. Just like having all my memories come at me at once was too much. It was like thinking sideways; everything came at me from directions I didn't know how to receive.

I reached up to my head again, this time gratified to feel something solid. I opened my eyes.

She watched me with the same impassivity in her bright gaze. Her eyes were pure light, the same as my body. But I didn't fool myself into thinking we were the same. She was more. She was so much more than I could even fathom.

"Oh my god," I whispered.

She leaned in. Her mouth cracked into what could be interpreted as a smile. "Indeed."

I took in a deep lungful of air, unsure if my lungs had even formed yet. Unsure even if I had lungs. Was air even necessary for light-people?

And still she, or I suppose She, gazed down at me, waiting patiently for my answer.

"Nia," I said. "I call myself Nia."

She scrunched up her nose and looked off in the distance as her fingers continued to work. It was deceptively human-like and made me feel comfortable. But then she focused those light-bright eyes on me again. I was dealing with someone, something, beyond my comprehension.

"Nia." She said my name. "Knee-ah." She pressed her tongue to the roof of her mouth with the consonant and then sighed on the vowel. "I don't like it."

My mouth, which was now fully formed, fell open at her pronouncement.

"But it's your choice." She shrugged. "Your free will." And then she scrunched her nose up again, as though she were repeating my name in her head and finding it just as distasteful.

"And you?" I asked. "What do I call you?"

"I find the need to name things fascinating."

Her fingers gave an upward tug, as though she were tying a knot. I felt the pull in my knee, like a doctor taking a rubber hammer to the joint to test reaction. My leg jerked, flexing and relaxing at her machinations. Then she moved her looming hands down to my toes.

"Just as I find it fascinating that most beings like

to have their essence cloaked in materials. I much prefer to roam in my natural state, but I've found it makes those around me uncomfortable. There was a time I didn't care, because caring and emotions weren't actual things. There was only instinct. But, at some point in time, my creations began pulling flesh around their light. It mutes their instincts."

I had nothing to say to that. Here I was talking to God. Maybe that wasn't the right word. She was the Creator, that much I knew from the return of my memories.

But my memories grew fuzzier as she knit skin over my light. I still remembered my mother's face, but the color from the scene and the details were fading. The stars in my mind dimmed, moved farther and farther away, beyond my reach.

"It's your flesh," she said, as though reading my mind, probably because she could. "Your skin suppresses your light. Like I said, most of my creations prefer skin. At first, I thought it had to do with the atmosphere of Heaven and the dust getting into your light. Most flora and fauna wear only their skins, but not mankind. From birth, human beings preferred to be swaddled in materials that further encase them and keep them separated from others. I've never quite understood it. And then you lot developed compassion to share the sensation with each other."

She shuddered. All I could do was stare.

"Eden," she said after a few seconds of silence.

"What?"

"That's what I prefer to be called," she said. "Eden. I also like Gaia and Ra. They're all soft sounds. I find that I like vowels. Very easy on the ears."

She reached up and tugged at her elongated ears. They were pointy at the top, like the renditions of elves in children's books.

"Funny little appendages," Eden said. "I wasn't quite sure what to do with them the first time they appeared. I started wearing them myself a few cycles ago. They balance out the head, don't you think?"

She wobbled her head left and right. Again, I could only stare mutely.

"The only true sense is touch. I didn't see the need to evolve beyond the tactical sense of touch. Light is simply a wave, which we experience as touch. Sound is just another wave, only it touches the ear. Smell, taste, sight, all are waves that touch us in different ways. It's redundant, really." She waved her hands as though brushing the notion aside. "But I allow my creations to explore and evolve in their own state of being. Up until a point, of course."

"Of course." It was all I could think to say. "So... you're God."

"Gah." Eden cringed. "I don't like that word. It's very harsh sounding." She shook her head as though she tasted something bad.

"But it's who you are?"

Eden shrugged. "I simply am. I never thought to question it. It's how it's always been. Since I was born."

"You were born?"

"I was born here." Eden lifted her slim arms to indicate the light surrounding us.

"Where are we exactly?"

"At the core of the planet, in its womb. Where all life began. My life happened to be the first life. Every life form that came after me likes to call me the Creator, but in reality, it was the planet that created us all. The Earth is our true god. But that comes off as abstract, and since I was born first, and engineered what came after me, all of creation looks to me."

I nodded in understanding, but my head was spinning with all the implications.

Eden held out her hand. At first, it was a solid

palm without lifelines. Then the flesh melted away. In the middle of her palm was a pool of swirling light. "Would you like to see it again?"

"See it? Again?"

"The birth of creation. I've shown you before."

I looked down at my hand. My fingers were now covered in skin. Thinly knit. Thin enough for the light to shine through.

I reached out to her hand, tentatively. I had no idea what I was afraid of. God was going to show me creation. It's what all scientists secretly dream of, a definitive answer to life's greatest question.

The moment my fingertips touched hers, I was pulled, yanked out of my skin. I don't know if my eyes were closed or open, but fire and heat and embers clouded my vision. Then, in an instant, the scene cleared and there was nothing but blue.

A blue so bright and soft at the same time it took my breath away. Earth. I'd always thought the planet was the most beautiful in the solar system. But this rendition of it, no print or satellite picture had ever come close to the Earth as seen in these waters.

The waters pulled into the Earth and it was like watching a National Geographic Special. Beautiful landscapes, growing flowers, grasslands, and seas teeming with life paraded through the waters of the cylinders like the opening of the *Lion King*. The Earth in all her majesty was on display.

"It takes precise chemistry to create the spark of life," said Eden. "I watched the seas and the first cells divide and multiply until they became what you call dinosaurs. I watched the first blade of grass grow until the first fairy stepped out of its roots. I watched primates stand up on straight spines and then discover fire. It's been most entertaining."

And then there was darkness. Eden had removed her hand from mine. My eyes had been closed. No light. Only the darkness of my eyelids.

"Ah, Nia." Eden's voice held a frown as she spoke the single harsh consonant in my name. "You're all done. Back in your skin."

I opened my eyes to the bright room. I rose to a sitting position. I was back in my own skin, and naked.

It hadn't dawned on me before that I was truly bare. I wasn't modest. But I felt weird being naked in front of God as a grown woman.

"I tried to keep to your original model." Eden admired her handiwork, cocking her head from side to side and squinting her large eyes. "How does it feel? Be honest. I can take criticism."

"I get the feeling you'd know if I wasn't honest."

Eden only smiled. An upward tilt of one side of her thin lips.

"I feel good as new." And I did. Better than new. There was a lightness about me. Though corporeal, I felt myself barely tethered to the platform.

"Good," said Eden. "Some beings are sentimental about their original skins. But all things must change."

I shifted on the platform, reaching my toes toward the white floor. The ground was solid, like marble, but warm. With both feet planted on the ground, I shifted and tried to stand. But the moment I was on my own, dizziness overcame me and I gripped the edge of the platform.

"My head hurts." I rubbed my temple, thankful it was solid this time.

"Those are your memories trying to fit themselves inside your head," said Eden. "You've been encased in a human body for thousands of cycles. These cavities were not designed to last so long or to hold the amount of memories you've acquired. A flaw in the design, I apologize. There's only so much space in the human ganglia."

I looked at her quizzically.

"Ganglia, the network of nerves that make the flesh of the body function. I believe mankind has taken to calling it brains. Such a funny word." Eden sniffed again, wrinkling her nose, her large eyes crinkling at the edges. "When the brain is confined inside your body cavity, it cannot access all your records, your memories, as it can in your natural state."

"My natural state? As a being of light."

She nodded.

"So, I am an angel?"

Eden smiled. "I've always liked that word. Ahn-gel. So soft."

"But I remember being born. I had a mother... and a father."

A father. I had a father. My brain ached at trying to reach deep into the recesses of my nerve network to pull up any memories of him.

"Mother. Father," said Eden. "Such human concepts. Though I do like the word daughter. It's soft but also strong. But mother?" She shuddered. "Such an invasion to have something inside of your body and then yanked out. The eggs and larvae were a good design with the reptiles and avians. But I was particularly fond of the grafting and seedling design of the flora."

My mother was dead. She'd been human. But

my father hadn't been. He was like me. Like Eden. "Where is my father?"

Eden tilted her head to the side, much like a bird listening for the presence of another. Her bright eyes glowed and then she refocused on me. "He's near."

"Does he know I'm here?"

Eden nodded.

I hesitated to ask to see him. He knew I was here. Why wasn't he waiting by my side when I woke up? Maybe he didn't care about me. Maybe he didn't want to be bothered with me.

In my mind, his face was hazy, his words muted. My mother had loved him, but I got the impression it was one-sided. What had Eden said about emotion? That caring and emotions weren't actual things.

But that was false. Emotions surged through my body like they had when my mother held me for the first time. I knew that emotion. It was love.

I was like my mother. I was capable of love. I had loved deeply in my life. And then my heartbeat quickened.

"Zane? Where's Zane?"

CHAPTER THREE

I took a moment and looked at my surroundings, realizing I was inside a structure. My eyelashes touched the tops of my cheeks as I blinked a couple of times. The white light that had dominated my vision gave way to yellow rock and red clay. Cabinets lined the perimeter. Inside the crevices of the shelves were creatures the likes of which I'd never seen before.

There was a bird-like creature, tall as a giraffe with a neck just as long. Except it had a beak like a parrot and the wings of a bat. There were creatures suspended in liquid, too. A pink jellyfish with a fat, opaque body. Inside its body was a worm-like creature that had a single dark eye. There was a cephalopod with rainbow-colored tentacles, its eyes vacant as its appendages swayed in the liquid.

"Those are the lost ones," said Eden. "Life forms that have gone extinct."

Her large eyes cast downward. Her lips bent in one direction and her brows creased in the opposite direction. The light in the room dimmed and the shadows fastened themselves around my shoulders.

I had never felt such intense sadness in my life. Now I understood her distaste of compassion. But I was still me, even inside a new body. I stepped away from Eden to investigate further.

There were also plants on display. Delicate sprouts with leaves that looked like hands. Vines with monstrous, bulbous heads that reminded me of Audrey II from *Little Shop of Horrors.* There were slender, reed-like blossoms with long blades that looked like legs and arms. The flowering bloom at the top of the staff looked more like a head than a bud.

Writings and diagrams floated in the air. The etchings were drawn not with ink or lead or pigment. They were penned with the same white energy that had permeated the room, the same energy in Eden's eyes.

Some of the symbols I recognized but my brain

had trouble deciphering the meanings. There were schematics of animals: invertebrates, fish, amphibians, reptiles, birds, and mammals. Also plants: mosses, ferns, gymnosperms, and angiosperms. Off to the side, there were combinations, various mixings of the groupings.

This was a science lab, filled with some of God's biggest hits and likely greatest failures. I guessed the creatures hanging in suspension were the failures, since none of them continued to walk or swim the earth. Which brought me back to my original question.

"What have you done with Zane?" I reached for the dagger perpetually at my hip and met only flesh. I was bare in more ways than one.

"The same as I did with you," said Eden. If she'd noticed that I'd reached for a weapon, she showed no concern. "I gathered his essence and made him a new skin."

"Then why isn't he here with me?" Zane would have never left my side while I was in danger. The man had fallen to his own death alongside me.

"Zayin's sire came to collect him some time ago."

"His sire?"

"You would use the word father, and I suppose in this instance it would be correct. Michael did lie with Zayin's mother and she conceived. Zayin's essence grew in her core and then she pushed him out through her vagina." Eden shuddered, distaste screwing her features. "Such an inefficient form of reproduction. I never adopted the practice myself."

She waved her hands in front of her bare torso. My eyes were drawn down to her non-existent genitalia. I cringed, shook my head, and looked away.

"I don't like that process or that word—vagina. One of my daughters calls it a hoo-ha. I do like the sound of that."

Eden sighed again, looking around at her schematics like this, the problem of vaginas and hoo-has, was a problem she wished to correct. Her gaze settled on an orb. It looked like a nucleus with swirling bits of energy of different shades circling around a core.

The orb took hold of my attention. I took a few tentative steps toward the orb. I reached out, but Eden's body came between my fingertip and the sphere.

"Ah ah," she chided. "Knock that down and you'll start the apocalypse."

But I couldn't take my attention away from it. "What is that?"

"The center of the earth. And the entire genetic library of existence."

I frowned at her, waiting for more of an explanation. None was forthcoming. I shook myself and took a step back, refocusing on the matter at hand. I needed to know that Zane was safe, intact, and whole again. The last time I'd seen him, felt him, he was dying in my arms, because of me.

There had to be a way out of here. I took a few tentative steps away from Eden. She didn't follow. Only watched me with that same impassivity, as though she were recording notes on my behavior for an experiment. That was likely true. She was the world's first scientist.

I found what looked like a doorway. There was no handle. It simply looked like a darker impression in the wall than the rest.

I reached my hand through it. It wasn't solid. The temperature shifted on the other side. It was markedly warmer on the outside.

I prepared to put my whole body through. I lifted my foot, but then noticed that my feet were bare. My gaze tracked up my legs and my torso.

I turned back to Eden. "Where are my clothes?"

"Discarded along with your original body."

It took a minute for my world to stand still after

those words. I didn't know what disturbed me more, that she'd thrown out my favorite boots or my body.

"Discarded?" I said.

"Hmm, I believe your flesh was thrown into the dragon pit as a snack."

Oh. Okay then. I supposed it wasn't a worse way to go than falling down a cavern. "Can I have something to cover myself?"

Eden cocked her head. "I gave you skin. Do you not like it? Is there a flaw in my design?"

"No," I said. "The body is fine. But if I'm going to go outside, where there are others, I want to cover myself."

Eden's brows pinched. "I will never understand this need of human beings. I've seen you cover other animals too. Little canines? They don't like it, you know. It's entirely unnatural."

"Please?"

She shrugged and raised her hand in acquiescence. Her fingers did that knitting motion again. Cotton formed around me out of thin air. But I knew it wasn't out of thin air. It was as though the material grew at her will. The fabric knitted over my skin, just as my flesh had moments ago, until my chest and torso were covered.

Creator she might be, but fashion designer she

was not. It was just a plain white sheath. There were straps over my shoulders and then the fabric hung down to just above my knees. But I was covered, and that was my goal.

I wasn't modest, but the hell if I was going to go out into the unknown without weapons or materials to cover my vulnerable spots.

"Are you ready now?" Eden asked.

I nodded.

She waved her hand, indicating that I should precede her out the doorway. I stepped through the opening and out into even more bright light. It felt like I stood close to the sun.

All around were stalactites and stalagmites. They were rusty red, sandy brown, and orange like the ripest fruit. Impossibly, between each of the pointy structures were grassy knolls and flowering bushes and tall trees. A stream of the clearest water meandered through the idyllic scenery.

The scene didn't make sense. It looked as though we were underground, in a barren desert, and in a lush oasis all at the same time.

"Where are we?" I asked.

"In the core of the earth."

That couldn't be possible. We should be burning up, eviscerated, if these were truly the temperatures of the core. The heat wasn't overbearing. It warmed me through, but not just my skin. It warmed the life essence inside of me. I stood for a moment, basking in it, feeling like it was charging me up like a battery.

"It would feel even better if you didn't have so many layers on," said Eden. "But to each his own. Come along… Nia."

She grumbled over my harsh-sounding name, but my attention focused on this whole new world I found myself in. My lips rounded in oohs and widened in ahhs as I took it all in. I ducked as something flew overhead. A pterodactyl.

"I kept specimens from all of the Earth's creatures, mainly for my records but also for nostalgia. I rather liked the Mesozoic Era."

"I thought the dinosaurs were wiped out by a comet that hit the Earth."

Eden chuckled. "I've heard that theory. Humans can be so imaginative."

"That's not what happened?"

"No," she said simply.

Her lips bent downward again with a touch of sadness. But not so great as when she'd gazed at the specimens she called the *lost ones*. Maybe the dinosaurs weren't exactly extinct. Not if there was a pterodactyl alive and well living below the Earth's surface.

It flew over a tree, flying close enough to touch its branches and making the tree sway. But the tree wasn't swaying, it was moving. Walking, to be exact. The arbor inclined the top of its branches as it passed me and Eden.

The tree wasn't the only thing that uprooted itself from the lush earth. Flowers rose, rising on petals to fly. The flowers and dinosaurs weren't the only things flying. There were beings of light flying. Angels. No. That wasn't the right term.

"Elohim," said Eden. "That's what we call ourselves."

Back on the surface, Elohim was used in the Bible as the name of God. But there was a great debate over the word because it was used in both the singular and the plural. Now I knew why.

"They're like you?" I said. "You all used to walk the earth."

These were Elohim, the original children of the earth. Beings of pure light. Before there was any firmament or water, there was fire and light. Like Eden, they came out of the light. I knew so much of this, but it was hard keeping it all straight now that my mind was encased in skin.

"That was a long time ago," said Eden. "I don't venture above any longer, not since the Ice Age. It's far too cold on the surface."

One Elohim swooped in close to us. Its body wasn't encased in skin, but its light had the shape of a human. Something about the way the being moved told me he was male. He, too, was naked, but had no genitalia.

I wrenched my gaze away. My cheeks heated, and I felt shame, though I'm not sure why. Another glance at his face told me that I should recognize him. Not his features, but there was something familiar about him.

He walked to Eden, more like marched to her. As he passed me, he spared me a single glance. His facial features weren't defined, but I would swear he sneered at me like I was something the saber-toothed tiger dragged in. I started to step back, but thought better of it. So instead, I held my ground even though my newly formed knees knocked.

"Ah, Michael," said Eden.

Michael? The man she said was Zane's sire? This was Zane's father.

Michael inclined his head to Eden. "Did you get what you needed from that one?"

Michael didn't acknowledge me this time, even though he was talking about me.

"I did, indeed," said Eden. "Her records were very detailed." She looked at me, a touch of admiration sparkling in her bright eyes.

But I wasn't dazzled. "Records? What records?"

"Shall we begin?" asked Michael. His attention never wavered from Eden. He continued to ignore me.

"I suppose it is time." Eden nodded and stepped toward him.

"Wait." I reached out but withdrew my hand before I actually yanked on God's arm.

"I have to get back to work now," she said.

Eden didn't turn back to me as she spoke. I'd been dismissed. It felt like a pat on the head by a father home late from work who was preparing to go into his home office and get back online.

"You'll find what you seek over there. We will talk again later, Nia."

And then she rose into the air along with Michael. Neither of them used wings. Eden let her skin fall away and dissipate into the atmosphere. She was nothing but light as she rose into the air.

I stared after them long after they were gone.

What records? What had Eden taken from me while I was dead?

Then I heard a familiar laugh, deep and filled with amusement and the love of life.

Zane faced me, but his attention wasn't on me. It was on a woman. He looked down at her with what I knew to be adoration. Jealousy stabbed my heart, so strong and so pure that I was certain I'd burst out of my skin.

CHAPTER FOUR

I didn't spontaneously combust. I stayed in my newly minted skin. A flood of memories pushed at the front of my brain with a force that nearly brought me to my knees. Each recollection burned clear and bright in my cramped mind, pushing aside what didn't matter, which was nearly every other thought, remembrance, and event in my life.

Zane.

He'd once told me we'd met eight times. Eight times since the beginning. I'd forgotten them during my long lifetime. With all my memories now stuffed inside my small brain, I feared I'd forget again. But that wasn't the case.

I remembered them. I remembered every single one of them. Inside my mind's eye, eight stars burned brightly.

The first time we'd met had been here. He'd sat in the fields. With a stele in his hand, he drew one of the flowers. The large, purple bloom had tilted its bulbous head over. Its velvety petals were as large as lily pads. Slowly the petals unfurled, each layer of purple getting lighter and lighter until its periwinkle interior showed. Inside that interior was a yellow stamen that blinked.

Four stamen-eyes blinked as the flowering plant regarded Zane's work. Zane allowed the bloom to study his work, watching its reaction with amusement. There was no mouth on the bloom to indicate approval or displeasure. There was no brow over the stamen to indicate surprise or boredom. After it looked its fill, it folded up the layers of petals and resumed its initial pose.

Zane smiled and repositioned his stele. Then, as though he felt the heat of my gaze on him, he turned his head and looked at me. The moment his eyes connected with mine I was pulled into another memory.

I walked out of the darkness this time. Wherever

I was, I came upon Zane's back again. This time he was standing over a fire with iron tools. There were scraps of animal hides covering his torso, but just barely. Zane had always been perfectly fine with nudity.

He hunched bare-chested over a beaded necklace. He worked the metal into a shape—the shape of my name. A U-shape with one of the tips slanted inward. He paused in his shaping, his ears twitching as though he sensed something. As he turned toward me, I was pulled away again.

This time, when I fell into the memory, I landed in his arms. My head nuzzled into that space below his chin and just above his heart, that space where I'd always fit perfectly. Neither of us were clothed this time. The weariness and silky satisfaction of an energetic bout of lovemaking had settled into my bones.

The moonlight shone through the structure and illuminated the pyramids outside. We could've been in Mesopotamia or Egypt. I wasn't entirely sure which memory this was. I remembered that we had been reunited in both.

We had a habit of breaking up. Not we. Me. I had a habit of leaving him. But never for long.

The last five hundred years we'd been together were all clear in my mind. My gaze fell upon the rising columns of ancient Greece while he worked on the original Parthenon and the statue of Athena. He painted bright colors, defying the Gothic style of the Dark Ages. He looked down at me with a twinkle in his eyes as he painted the ceilings of the Sistine Chapel.

Even though there were eight bright spots in the galaxy of my memories, that same twinkle in his eyes always glimmered in every direction in the darkness of my mind. In my star chart of memories, he was always there.

He was always there. Even when we weren't together, he was always near. I knew that, had always known that.

Zane was the one constant in my life. He called me his True North, but he'd always been my anchor. The one thing I could hold on to.

And, time and time again, I'd let him go.

When I did, whenever I did, I floundered. Like falling through the darkness of space until we came back together again. But now, as he smiled brightly down at this female standing before him in the Garden of Eden, I wondered if perhaps I'd been too late this time.

It had always been me who'd let go. Zane hadn't reached out this last time I'd left. Except when I fell to my death. Now that our lives were put back together in new bodies, maybe things had changed for him.

Zane had told me there had only ever been me in his heart while we were on Earth. But what about before we'd come up to the surface? Had he left someone behind down here?

Even if this woman wasn't new, maybe he was tired of me constantly leaving him. I'd made him chase me for so long, longer than any man in history likely. I'd been with his best friend, for god's sake.

Zane and I weren't back together right now. We'd only just become friends again in the last few moments of our lives. I knew he loved me. I didn't doubt that, never had. He had to know that I loved him. That had never been in question. Maybe that wasn't enough anymore.

Lightheaded, I blinked the stars of my mind away and focused on the bright smile of the man before me. My belly tightened with nausea, though empty of any food or water. But then, like the magnets that we were, his gaze lifted, and he found me.

His eyes widened. His nostrils flared. The edges

of his lips, which had broadened in a smile for the other woman, stretched even wider as he audibly exhaled. His gaze roamed over my form from my head to my toes. Like always, I held still for him as he took me in, but only for a few seconds.

Zane stepped around the woman and headed toward me. I realized belatedly that I was already in motion toward him. This time when we came together, I met him more than halfway.

He came to me, naked as the day he was born. Or rather, reborn. Nudity was a constant companion to this man. And why wouldn't it be? Zane was magnificent.

From his long feet that anchored his powerful thighs to his impressive manhood that, even while flaccid, still caused women to gasp. The happy trail below his belly button urged my eyes south, but I forced them up his defined chest to his face.

He stopped abruptly as we came toe to toe. We were a hair's breadth apart, but he didn't take me into his arms. His eyes scanned me, every inch, like he was making a memory or looking for an imperfection. Most likely the latter.

Zane was an artist. I was his favorite subject. He knew my features better than most.

"How did she do?" I asked.

"Who?"

"Eden?"

His smile widened even more, his head tilted as though to regard me from a different angle. "I didn't think the original could be improved upon. I stand corrected. She changed the slope of your cheek…"

He reached out his hand. My breath caught as the tips of his fingers came closer and closer, their heat preceding the impact. But his fingers halted just before they got to my skin.

We were standing barely an inch apart from each other, but still not touching. I ached to be in his arms. I knew the moment I got there, there would be a ninth spark, a new star to join the other eight. That last spark would ignite into the biggest and brightest star in my memory, and it would be the last. The last time we'd meet, because after all that we'd been through, I was never letting this man go again.

My gaze tracked to that space just below his chin and above his heart, that space that fit me so well. Something told me not to make a dive for that spot, even though it was mine. But damn if it wasn't hard holding still during the wait.

In the end, Zane lowered his hand. His fingers fell to his sides. Inside my soul, the spark fizzled to an ember. A huge wave of disappointment washed over me.

"How are you feeling?" he asked.

"Fine," I lied. "You?"

"I feel whole now that I've seen you."

And just like that, a glow emitted from the dim light of ashes inside the pit of my stomach. I reached out to him, preparing to temper the fever between us. Before my fingertips made it across the inch-wide gulf between us, Zane leaned back just out of my reach. I yanked my hand back from the burn.

Zane winced when he saw the hurt and rejection in my eyes. But he didn't reach for me. He kept his distance.

So, we weren't all right. Even though our bodies were put back together, even though our spirits were renewed, the two of us were still broken.

Zane sighed as he met my gaze. There was more gold in his eyes than I remembered. Probably because his skin had just been reknitted over his soul. When he looked at me, it was with every bit of love and adoration that I had felt for the millennia we'd known each other. So why was there this distance?

He opened his mouth, likely to explain, but before he could speak, someone else did. I hadn't noticed the woman he'd been looking adoringly at had moved closer. I prepared to throw my ire on her, but froze.

"Theta?" said the mystery woman.

I couldn't get any air in my lungs, though again, I wasn't entirely certain if breathing was necessary beneath the surface. It was just habit.

The form came closer. I wanted to shake my head to clear the fog, because I couldn't believe my eyes. The woman looked like she could be my sister. She had the same dark hair, the same honey-brown features, even the same tilt to her eyes.

"Vau?" My voice croaked with grief and pain and disbelief and hope.

The woman nodded, but the confirmation rocked me back on my heels.

I still couldn't accept the possibility that it was true. My own rebirth? Sure, no problem. Zane being alive and whole? Absolutely. But my oldest and dearest friend?

"Vau?" I had to ask again, because it simply couldn't be her.

"It's me," she said.

And it was her. It was her too-big smile. It was that glint of wonder in her wide eyes. She stood before me, whole and happy and alive. I didn't wait for permission as she stood before me. I enveloped her into my arms and went stiff at the impact.

It was like a near-death experience. My life flashed before my eyes. But then I realized it wasn't my life. It was Vau's.

Weakness flooded through my veins; my immortality leached out of me and humanity set in. It was the same as when I'd fallen to my death, tumbling over rocks and impacting on the bottom of the cavern.

Only Vau had been lying on a slab as her life was stolen. She hadn't fallen; she'd been held down. Shards pierced her skin, but not from the walls of a cave. They were in the hands of men. Her screams tore from my raw throat. And then there was darkness.

"Oh, Theta. Theta, I'm so sorry."

I was on my knees, grabbing fistfuls of the warm earth. My head spun, and I tried to release the hold of the nightmarish visions. When I opened my eyes, Vau and Zane were crouched around me. Both outstretched their hands but neither touched me.

"What was that?" I asked. "What just happened?"

Vau reached out to me, and I flinched. Slowly, her fingers advanced. Instead of touching my skin, she let the curtain of my hair that fell over my face glide through her hand.

"Your skin is still thin," said Vau. "It's easy to share my light with you."

"I saw you die. I felt the torment."

"I know," Vau soothed. She slid my hair out of my face and tucked it behind my ear, careful not to touch the skin at the cone of my ear. "I'm sorry. I figured Eden would've warned you. You'll learn to control it in time as your skin thickens."

A hand came onto Vau's shoulder. Brown fingers gave her a squeeze. I looked up into the face of Epsilon. He was here too. Alive and well.

"Hello, Theta," he said. "It's good to see you."

The last time I'd seen him, I'd been angry with him for breaking Vau's heart. It had always irked me that we'd parted on bad terms and had never patched things up before he died. My instinct was to run into his arms, but I did not want a second showing of a friend's death today. And so I gave him a weak smile as I put both my feet under me.

Vau rose and stood inside of Epsilon's embrace. I stood on my own, though my legs were as shaky as a new fawn's. Beside me, Zane's hands were balled into fists at his sides. Was that why he didn't reach out to me? What didn't he want me to see from his past?

"There's so much to catch up on," said Vau. "But it will have to wait until later. Here comes our father."

Our father? As in Vau's and my father? *Our father?* As in he was here? Vau focused over my shoulder. I turned and prepared to meet my maker.

CHAPTER FIVE

No one was there. No, wait, that wasn't entirely true. The air was hazy, like a mirage in the desert.

The air felt different. The atmosphere felt heavy, saturated. Like walls were closing in on me, but I was outside.

Something was coming closer. A light grew from the hefty haze. Brighter and brighter as it came toward me. The brilliance didn't hurt, but I wanted to shield my eyes out of respect.

I didn't lift my hands to cover my gaze. Nor did I shut my eyes. I couldn't look away.

The blaze of light grew and grew. The rays reached outward, just far enough in front of me that I could reach out and touch. Close enough that the heat singed the raised hairs on my wrists, which I pulled against my body to protect my heart.

The light coalesced, and a being stepped out. The light being formed limbs and took on a human shape. Skin knitted over the light, encasing the glowing warmth inside a fleshy shell.

The knitting began at the fingertips and toes. The pattern cross-stitched up the forearms and shins. Like with Eden and Michael, the groin area was that of a doll. Just a bump of sexless flesh.

I was looking at my father's junk—even though it wasn't junk. That's when I finally shut my eyes.

But only for a second. I urged them back open the very next instant, unwilling to miss anything. When I looked again, it was at my father's face.

Features formed. His skin was the color of the volcanic earth, more a ruddy red than an earthen brown. His chin was a rounded triangle with a dimple, like the backside of a shovel. His nose was long and concave; at the end it turned up. He was hairless; the same nodes and knots decorated the top of his crown in a beautiful swirling pattern that my fingers itched to touch. The hard line of his mouth instructed me to keep my hands to myself.

My memories of my mother showed me a woman who I favored physically. Looking at my father was not like looking into a mirror. My father's features weren't familiar to me. We looked absolutely nothing alike. But we favored each other. We didn't share the same features, but we shared the same energy.

We stared at each other. Neither of us said anything. Vau broke the silence.

"Theta, this is Gabriel, our sire."

Gabriel. My father's name was Gabriel. It was such a normal human name. The name had been written about in many religious texts. Gabriel appeared in the Jewish, Christian, and Islamic scriptures. He was credited with being a messenger who explained the visions of some prophets and foretold the births of others. I wondered if the prophet and my father were the same being.

"Hi, Dad." I waved and offered him a smile.

The skin over Gabriel's right eye crinkled. His mouth remained in an expressionless line. So, I didn't get my eyebrows, my eye color, or my sense of humor from my father.

"You may call me Gabriel." His voice reminded me of the sound of an African djembe drum. The start of the words hit with a staccato beat and then resonated down in the belly of the hollow instrument. "You have chosen the name of Theta?"

"No, actually, I'm—I go by Nia these days."

Gabriel nodded. His large eyes scrutinized me. I fidgeted under his gaze. As I searched for something to say, there was movement behind me, and I turned.

Vau stepped back toward Epsilon. "We'll give you two some time alone," she said.

It had been centuries since we'd last been in each other's presence, but she knew me well. She knew my alarmed features screamed a distress call. And if that wasn't enough, I mouthed the word *no*. This little reunion between father and daughter was painful with just the two of us. She couldn't leave us on our own.

But Vau tilted her head in a call to put my *subligaculum* on. Problem was I hadn't worn loincloths since the invention of the chemise as an undergarment. I scrunched my face in a plea, but Vau only narrowed her eyes at me. I wanted to stomp my foot and call her a terrible older sister.

"I'll find you later," she said, tilting her head meaningfully toward our father. Then she linked hands with Epsilon and headed away.

They walked past Zane, who watched me. My distress reflected in his eyes. His body leaned forward, preparing to come to my aid. But then his gaze flicked over my shoulder.

I didn't turn. I watched Zane. His jaw tensed along with his fists. Resignation stole across his face.

His eyes found mine again. They pierced mine. Warmth flooded me, strengthened me. But it wasn't enough. I needed him by my side. I needed his arms around me. I needed him to stay.

Zane gave me a shake of his head. Though he wanted to stay, he couldn't. His eyes narrowed, as if to tell me that though he had to step away from me, he wouldn't be far. He'd never been far from me. That relaxed me and loosened my anxiety. Somewhat.

Zane took one step back, then another. He didn't break eye contact with me until I nodded. Then with one final glance, he turned and took the strides to catch up with Vau and Epsilon, leaving me alone with my father.

I faced Gabriel's imposing figure. I wasn't afraid of him. I just was unsure what was about to happen. Or how I was supposed to behave.

He stared at me. I searched for something to say. But my one and only try had bombed, so I remained mute and waited for his direction. After all, he'd been radio-silent in my life for thousands of years.

"You have your dame's eyes," he said. "I'd forgotten what her eyes looked like."

That bass drum of his voice thumped through my ears and vibrated the memories in my head. I tried to pull one from the tightly packed cluster in my head, but it wouldn't budge.

"No," Gabriel said. "That is not true. I never forget anything. I simply had not thought of her eyes in a few thousand cycles."

I wanted to be angry with him. He hadn't thought about my mother? Well, I had. I'd thought about her every day. I'd thought about them both. I'd lain awake at night wondering if, in fact, I had parents. Or if I was just some abnormal thing that had sprung fully formed into the world.

I'd seen my mother's face in my mind. And now that my head was stuffed with thousands of years of memories, I had trouble pulling the details of her from the pile.

I could see that Gabriel wasn't having the same difficulty. His bright gaze went dim as he looked off into the distance. Was he remembering her? Did he see her clearly? Instead of getting angry, I got hungry.

"I can't remember," I said. My voice sounded like the whine of a toddler. "I want to, but it's too fuzzy in my head."

Gabriel blinked and focused his golden eyes on

me. As though he could hear the grumble in my belly, the grumble that wished to be fed the visions in his head, he held out his palm to me. The skin I'd watched knit itself together unknitted to reveal a pool of light in his hand, like he was holding water. He wanted me to touch that spot, but I hesitated.

Experiencing Vau's unfiltered memories had brought me to my knees. But that had been my fault for not knowing how to handle the light. When I'd touched Eden's palm, I'd only seen what she'd wanted to show me. I had to assume Gabriel would take the same care.

He watched me, in that impassive way I was coming to remember was the Elohim's. Offering me information and waiting to see what I'd do with it. I lifted my hand and reached out one finger.

The moment my fingertip touched the light of his palm, my knees went weak, but I didn't fall to the ground. I thought it was jam-packed in my head? Touching Gabriel's palm was like walking through a tornado to get inside a hurricane.

"Focus," he said. I wasn't sure if he said it into my ears or thought directly into my mind.

I tried again. And then I saw her. My mother, through his eyes. My mother's eyes, shining bright. They looked off in the distance, at him. In his memories, Gabriel turned, and when his gaze fell upon her, I felt her breath catch in my chest.

As he looked closely at the memory, something sparked inside Gabriel's eye. His left eye twitched as though it saw something bright that he had to shield himself from. I sensed he couldn't name the emotion, but I could. It wasn't passion. It was curiosity.

I knew the emotion well. I got it every time I discovered something I didn't know, something that intrigued me.

Gabriel's memories flickered in slideshow fashion after that first one. I watched my mother through my father's eyes. I watched each memory slide by, and with each flicker, my mother fell deeper and more hopelessly in love with Gabriel. I watched Gabriel try to mimic the actions of emotions. He tried, but he failed.

He didn't love her. He didn't know how. In the end, he simply tried to make her comfortable and content.

I saw her belly full, and then Vau.

I saw her belly full again, and then me.

I saw my mother wither and grow old. And then she was gone. I watched as Gabriel gently laid her body in the molten lava at the center of the Earth. As her body dissolved in the flames, his left eye twitched again. Then he closed both his eyes and turned away.

I yanked my hand away. My gaze was accusatory. Gabriel still looked at me impassively. His memories were clear, but he may as well have forgotten about her.

"She lived the equivalent of three hundred years," he said. "That is the longest the human body can hold the light."

Somehow I knew that what he'd shared had been less than a fraction of what was inside of him. To him, my mother was only a second in his life. Vau and I were mere moments to a being as timeless as him.

"Why am I here?" I asked. "Why did you have me and Vau, and the others?"

"It's tedious work for Elohim to be on the surface monitoring the affairs of the creatures the Earth produces. We began creating the Ishim, hybrids of the apex predators of the Earth and the light within us. During the time of the dinosaurs. The first were the dragons. During the time of the flora, there were the fae. And when the apes stood and claimed dominance, we made you twelve. Your jobs were to report back on the progress of life on the surface..."

"You had children to keep an eye on humanity?"

Not because he wanted to continue his bloodline, not that he had any blood. Not because he wanted to see himself in the new life, even though we looked nothing alike physically. He'd had children to do his grunt work?

Gabriel nodded. "Now you are returned, you'll give your testimony."

He turned his back and that was the end of the conversation. His skin faded and his light shone through his thin flesh. He was preparing to take off, but I wasn't done yet.

"Wait. What do you mean *testimony?*"

He didn't pause. His voice came from the slowly fading space. I knew for certain his lips didn't move this time. "Your experience of humanity will help determine the future of the life forms. Some of the things the Earth creates are not for the good of all."

"Wait? What does that mean, *some of the things aren't good for all?*"

Gabriel paused then, his light flickering. He tilted his head as though to punctuate the question mark.

"Are you saying that certain kinds of people are bad?" Holy crap, was my dad a racist?

"No, not some kinds of people."

A wave of relief flooded through me.

"The entire race of mankind."

My mouth worked but nothing came out except the whistle of the W sound as I tried and failed to ask any of the five W's: who, what, where, when, why.

"Based on the memories and experiences collected from the five Ishim who have returned," he continued, "it appears the human experiment is a failed one. We are debating the fate of mankind now. I need to return to my work."

The air left my lungs. Before I could refill them to utter a single word, Gabriel's flesh completely fell away. He became pure light and dissipated right before my eyes.

"Hey," I called out to the thin air. "Gabriel?" I shouted into the void. But there was no response.

I pursed my lips together so they didn't wobble. A hot wind blew past me, and I couldn't shake the feeling that I was a child that had been lost at a crowded mall, left behind at an amusement park and my parents had entirely abandoned me.

CHAPTER SIX

I stared at the place where Gabriel dissipated for long moments after the air and his life's energy had cleared. God and her angels were debating the fate of mankind, and the deciding vote might come down to my memories.

Crap.

That did not bode well for humanity. My experiences were a mixed bag when it came to the human race. I'd seen them at their highest heights, but I'd been a victim of their lowest lows. Even worse, I spent my life cataloguing the highs, lows, and in-betweens because of my firm belief that all stories, even the ugly ones, should be told.

Crap.

If only Eden had told me she downloaded my

memories as she knitted me a new body. If the Elohim had a bit of context for what they would see in my head, then perhaps I could sway them toward leniency for mankind. Maybe it wasn't too late. If I could just figure out where they all had gathered.

The air shifted. I thought for a second that maybe Gabriel might've come back. I held my breath, and my belly fluttered at the possibility that my dad had returned for me. I looked up and then had to duck.

A massive beast flew above me. Its body was snake-like in its sinewy length. But unlike a snake, it had limbs; four clawed feet extended out from its torso. Two more appendages grew from its back and extended into wings. The creature turned its narrow head toward me and looked down with the brownish-golden eyes of a tiger. It huffed, and puffs of smoke rose around its snout.

Dragon.

It was the color of emeralds. In fact, its skin looked as tough as emeralds, with the same twinkling sparkle that made women catch their breath while staring at the jewels. I was dumbfounded at its beauty, awestruck by the intelligence in those tiger-eyes.

The dragon turned away, but I still felt the heat

of someone's gaze. And that's when I saw her. A woman rode on the dragon's back.

She wore battle armor with pale blue breastplates and golden epaulettes. Her boots were white leather with a sturdy black stem. I tugged at the plain white fabric that covered my body, and my stomach twisted with envy at her stylish ensemble.

Dark braids flew behind her head, slapping at her pointed ears and wrapping around the sword holstered at her back. She looked down on me as she flew past. Her golden eyes scanned my simple dress and bare feet. She quirked a dismissive brow, then with a curl of her lip, she gave the dragon a kick to urge it on and they darted out of my sight like I was beneath her notice.

What the hell?

For the first time I noticed the other beings milling about. Tree people, flower people, light people. But no one seemed to think the presence of a dragon ridden by a woman ready for battle was anything out of the ordinary. It probably was ordinary. Beings of light, trees with legs, flying dinosaurs. All that was left for me to witness was a man walking on water.

There was no man standing on the stream that cut through the lush foliage. But someone was there.

Eden cradled a plant in her arms. The plant turned its head and opened its petals to reveal stamen eyes. Both god and bud stared at me with interest.

I walked over to Eden. She bent down on her haunches, moving aside soil with one hand as she cradled the plant being with the other.

"I've looked at your memories," said Eden.

"That quickly?" I asked.

"Time moves different down below than it does above. Though it bends to my will."

Eden looked to the plant. It looked from me, to her, then to the hole in the ground. It wrapped its roots around Eden's forearm and nestled its bulbous head into her thin flesh.

"You can bend time?" I asked.

Eden waggled her head. "I don't bend it. I bend myself. Slow down my vibration until I move through the cracks of the seconds."

She carefully extracted the plant's limbs from her arm. The bud of the flower rubbed against her wrist one last time, leaving a yellow dust of pollen on her flesh.

"Go on now," Eden said.

The petals drooped, but the plant did as Eden commanded it. With its roots, it stepped gingerly into the soil. Eden pushed the dark earth over the roots as though she were tucking the plant in for the night.

I watched, fascinated. It was such a motherly thing to do. She was Mother Earth, after all.

"About my memories..." I began.

"You've been digging all your life," she said. "Do you suppose it was because you were homesick to get back down here?"

"I..."

"Such an interesting phrase? Are you sick from being away or are you sick to get back from whence you came?" Eden brushed the dirt off her hands and stood.

"Humans thought hell was below earth," I said. "No one wants to come down here. But this place is like Iceland."

"Iceland?" Eden shivered. "I don't much like the cold."

"It's not cold in Iceland. It's actually green and lush."

"Then why is it called Ice Land?"

"They call it Iceland so no one wants to come there."

Eden cocked her head in that birdlike fashion. Then she nodded. "Yes, I suppose that sounds like something a human would do."

"Eden? Are you going to wipe them out of existence?"

"Humans, you mean," she said. "There is so much strife above ground. Wars, brutality, anguish, despair. Some Elohim believe it would be a mercy to end all the suffering."

"Not everyone is suffering," I insisted. "And it's only a few who cause it."

"How was your meeting with your father?" asked Eden.

I jerked back from whiplash. She seemed to have a knack for that, changing the topics of conversation. I wondered if it might be ADHD. She had the whole history of the world in her mind.

"Don't you already know?" I said. "Don't you see all?"

"I don't see all. But I eventually know all. Everyone wants to tell me everything that's happened to them. I suppose I have one of those faces."

She tilted her head left and right, framing her face with her slim fingers and batting her lashes, for my observation.

"I see patterns," she continued. "There's a pattern with offspring and their sires. Children seem to think that if they come from your loins then you owe them something."

"Well. Yeah. Don't you?"

"I was born fully formed. I have no mother or father. There was nothing before me. I've been alive for over four billion cycles around the sun. I woke up in a sea of magma at three hundred degrees. I was alone and small. All around me was vastness. I pulled a membrane around my light and absorbed nutrients. I continued to live instead of being pulled back into the primordial sea. One day, I was tired of being alone and I replicated myself. I made the Elohim. First Michael, and then Gabriel, and then the others. And I was no longer alone."

So, the creation myths had a basis of truth. We came from the body of a woman, though maybe not her rib.

"I don't owe them anything. They expect nothing from me."

"And you kept creating life from there?" I asked.

"Some." She nodded. "But I didn't have this much imagination."

She indicated the vast array of beings milling about the caverns and pathways of the underground paradise. There were Elohim, flora of various sizes and colors, reptiles with long necks and feathers, mammals with two heads and six legs.

"I watched meteorites shower the earth," Eden continued. "Out of the destruction came a diversity of life that I could have never dreamed up. Not that I have dreams. I don't even sleep. It seems a waste of time. But I think dreaming might help me in my creations."

I hadn't seen many of these creatures roaming around on Earth. There were no records or drawings of hardly any of them. Overhead, the dragon circled and weaved through the stalactites.

"Eden? What happened to the dinosaurs?"

"Hmm? Oh. They rebelled. Not all of them. Only the dragons."

I waited for her to say more. Her gaze wasn't on me. Though she was present, standing beside me, I barely held her attention. Her eyes were far away. Her eyelids hung low, like she was almost sad.

"They were such beautiful creatures," she said. "Some of my most lovely work. You've seen the bones, I know. Even their insides were lovely, yes. I hated to lose them."

"Did you get rid of them?"

Her golden gaze focused on me. "No. I can't bear

destruction of the living. I've seen so much death in my life. I'm a creator, not a destroyer."

"But they were destroyed."

"There was a war. In the heavens." Her gaze tilted toward the surface.

"Earth was invaded by aliens?"

Eden cocked her head as she gazed at me. "Such an imagination. No. It was Michael."

Michael?

Then war broke out in heaven. Michael and his angels fought against the dragon, and the dragon and his angels fought back. But he was not strong enough, and they lost their place in heaven. The great dragon was hurled down—that ancient serpent called the devil who leads the whole world astray. He was hurled to the earth, and his angels with him.

"The dragons rebelled?" I said. "And Michael killed them all?"

"Not all. I saved some." Her head tilted back to regard the mighty beast that flew above us.

"Why didn't you just stop the rebellion?"

She turned to me, large eyes bright. In this warm place at the center of the Earth, a chill went down my spine. "They turned away from me, their own mother. There was so much destruction and waste of lovely species. I couldn't save them all. Afterwards, I brought on the Ice Age. The fae left for a warmer realm and life started over. Apes rose and gave birth to humanity. A fresh start. It was better that way."

"Now you're thinking of destroying your children all over again," I said.

"I've given warnings—floods, famine, disease. Just like with the dragons. But like the dragons, humanity isn't paying heed. The pattern is repeating. Even worse this time. Humans have spread over the earth like a disease. I saw from your memories that they've destroyed the seas, dumping refuse into the waters. They've polluted the sky, burned a hole in the atmosphere. I saw from Zayin's memories that children can't breathe the air in parts of the world. I can hear the suffering of animals down here. Am I supposed to allow the whole world to suffer at mankind's whim?"

I opened my mouth to protest but nothing came out. Eden cocked her head to the other side as she gazed at me. It felt like I was under an X-ray.

"You seem to have the notion that the world is a clock, and I the clockmaker. Some great mechanic. You think the world is a machine and that if only we could find the part that is broken, dig it up, root it out, then we can fix it."

Well, yeah. That made perfect sense to me. Like

broken bones uncovered or an artifact whose date was hard to place, you had to only piece things together to get a clear picture.

"That's where you are so wrong, Nia. The world is a system. We're all connected. What happens above affects those of us below. Michael tells me some humans are playing with atoms." She shook her head in a tsking fashion. "Even without their explosives, they've caused the extinction of hundreds of my creations in the last five hundred cycles. If humanity is allowed to go on this way, it could be the end to us all. It's my worst nightmare, and I do not dream."

"But... but..." I felt like a kid trying to argue against an unfair punishment. I'd only been in the vicinity of the mischief. I hadn't planned or partaken of any of the raucous behavior, but I still felt the blow of the lash. "You've saved everything that ever lived. Now you're going to purposely eradicate a whole species. It's not right. It's not fair."

Yes, that was my argument. The good old *the world is unfair* argument. And just like with human parents, it wasn't going to fly with God.

"Maybe not," said Eden. "But it may bring balance. You'll come to see that I'm right. Not now, but maybe in a few centuries or a millennium. You should be excited. You'll get to be a part of something new. You can record from the beginning."

Eden brushed her hands on her sides. The dirt had long since fallen from her flesh and her hands were wiped clean.

"I have to get back to work," she said.

Before I could launch another lame argument, Eden dissipated.

CHAPTER SEVEN

I walked aimlessly around through paradise. The wonders ceased to amaze me after the anticlimactic meeting with my dad and the pre-apocalyptic run-in with Eden. I was headed nowhere, so of course my feet led me to him.

Zane sat in a pasture not far away from where Gabriel and I had talked. He'd stayed near. All my long life, he'd never been so far he couldn't reach out to me.

He sat on a mound of colorful grass, sketching. But there was no parchment before him, no brush in his hand. Instead, he'd peeled the skin of his fingertip away and was drawing in the air with his light. I couldn't make out the sketch from this distance, so I moved closer.

As my footsteps carried me to him, all anxiety and urgency for the plight of humanity left me. My most pressing desire was to climb into Zane's lap, to be wrapped in his arms and drowned in his kisses. It had been so long since we'd kissed. My belly grumbled for an entirely different reason.

I lifted my foot to take a step, but something held me back from running and diving into Zane's chest. I moved forward, but slowly. As I approached him from behind, his shoulders tensed.

It was slight. I'm sure I only noticed it because I knew him so well. He never tensed when I came near him. Well, unless we were fighting. Were we fighting?

My steps halted as I stood rooted in uncertainty. I settled down just beyond his reach, folding my legs into a pretzel as my butt hit the soft ground. I opened my mouth to speak, but something caught in my throat and I clamped my lips shut.

"The first time I saw you," Zane said, "was just over there."

He pointed to a field of purple blooms. The memory came to me instantly. Memories of him separated easily from the mass now. Plus, I'd touched this sight not too long ago.

They were the same flowers with the huge bulbous heads from my memory. The ones I'd seen when I'd woken up from death. Most of the flowering heads remained closed as their stems shifted in a breeze I didn't feel. A few of the petals were open and a couple of stamens blinked. I turned my gaze back to Zane.

"Zane? Are we still not okay?"

He was facing away from me. When he turned back a frown creased his brows. "We're fine."

The space between his shoulder blades called to me. Comfort and peace waited for me in those broad shoulders, and I wanted so desperately to reach out and grab it after all that we'd been through. My hands balled into fists in my lap.

"Why won't you let me touch you?" I asked.

His head dipped. He turned enough so that his chin touched the top of his shoulder. "Touch, in this place, is different."

So, I was right. There was something Zane didn't want me to see from his past. When Vau had touched me, I'd seen her memories, more than I'd wanted to see. When Gabriel had touched me, his vast knowledge overwhelmed me, and then I felt all his feelings, or lack thereof, when he showed me his memories of my mother.

"Just tell me what it is you don't want me to know," I said. "It won't change anything."

"You think I'm hiding something from you?"

I lifted my chin to bounce my head up and down in a nod, but something stopped me. The only things Zane had ever hidden from me were things about my past. My eyelids felt heavy as I realized the truth. It wasn't his memories he was afraid of.

"I can't change anything I've done in the past," I said.

"I'm not asking you to change anything. I just..." He trailed off as he finally turned and faced me. His gaze narrowed. His head cocked to the side in observation, but the pupils of his eyes darted here and there as they regarded me. I knew that look.

"Don't move," he said.

"No." I shook my head and held up my index finger. "Don't you dare."

"Just one second, *mon petit coeur.*"

I huffed out a breath, knowing I'd lost his full attention. He got this way whenever he saw something beautiful that he wanted to capture with his art. Zane was a man obsessed when it came to his craft.

He reached up to the sketch he'd done with his energy. The yellow mist came back into his hand.

Then he turned and began to sketch my face using the energy of his very soul.

"When did you learn to do that?" I asked.

He shrugged. "Probably before, when I lived here. I just remembered how."

His essence left his fingertip as he drew the outline of my face. Two fine lines formed the half crescents of my left eye, then another two for my right. Thicker lines of energy formed my upper lip.

"Zane? You don't need to draw me. Not if you're going to look at me forever."

"I am going to look at you forever. Don't move."

Don't move.

How many times had this man said those words to me?

Don't move.

He'd said them while painting me, sculpting me, making love to me, presenting me with a surprise, and even trying to save my life.

Don't move.

And what had I done? I'd fidgeted from my inability to hold still. I'd shifted positions to make things better for myself. I'd walked away from him to satisfy some selfish part of myself.

Yet here he was, painting my portrait with a piece of his soul. Oh, the irony. And now he was so close but so far. He didn't want to touch me because he didn't want to see my past, namely the other man I'd welcomed into my arms.

"I'm sorry," I said, but my voice was barely above a whisper, laden with shame.

Zane's finger paused. He didn't ask me to clarify. I probably couldn't remember all the things I needed to apologize for when it came to him.

"I would've taken that fall for you," he said. "I would've shoved you into Tresor's arms if it meant you'd live. I would've let you go."

I shook my head, countermanding his edict yet again to stay still. "I don't want to be in a world without you. If you'd jumped, I'd have come in after you."

I shifted closer. I couldn't help myself. When I did, my forehead brushed the outline he'd drawn of my face. My nose was in the thick of the markings of his spirit.

When my flesh met his, Zane's memories washed through me like a fine wine on a warm summer's night. There was a riot of colors and patterns and textures and me. My face was everywhere in his thoughts, in his dreams, in his reality.

He gazed down at me as I slept. He laughed with

me as we strolled along the bank of a river. He watched over me as I reached into the earth to extract an artifact.

He was there. His arms wrapped around me. He stood beside me. His silhouette kept watch in the shadows.

He didn't need to pretend or approximate emotions. They were all there. Clearly written on his face, and if I didn't see them clearly enough, he'd drawn them out on parchment, etched them in stone.

I breathed in the last bits of his soul. His heart was on the tip of my tongue. When I opened my eyes, his gaze was on my lips.

I closed my mouth and swallowed the energy he'd used to draw me so he would always remain inside me. I felt possessive as his essence slid down my throat. Some bits came to rest in my gut, but most took root in my heart where he belonged.

And all the while he stared. Until finally, he scooted closer. Just an inch. But it brought us to within a hair's breadth of kissing.

It took everything in me to hold still and wait for him. It had to be his decision, his move. My move had been clear. I was all in.

Zane took a deep breath. Then he reached out

his finger, the one with the tip still exposed. His hand shook as it approached my cheek. I held still for him. Mostly.

"I love you," I said.

The tremble in his hand stopped. A smile spread across his lips. His gaze connected with mine. "I know."

His touch was a gentle blast against my face. Just the tip of a single fingertip traced the outline of my cheek and caused a tender earthquake.

A few of my memories trickled through, mainly of us together. There was the first time I'd seen him, when I'd come up behind him on this grassy knoll. Then every first time we met after that. Looking back on it now, it was inevitable that we'd end up here, right back where we began.

More memories shuddered through. We were together in Mesopotamia, in Egypt, in Asia. Together with Vau and Epsilon, with Scully and Diaz. The two of us standing with Tres. And then me alone with Tres.

I tried to pull back, to shut that particular door. But Zane had seen. He gritted his teeth when the more intimate parts flashed of my time with Tres. Instead of trying to control my past and hide the uncomfortable truths, I put it all on the table.

There would be no more secrets between us. There would be no more hiding. I knew exactly what my future looked like from this moment on.

Zane looked in my eyes and saw that truth. A second, then a third fingertip touched my cheek. His palm cupped my chin.

My heart raced, and my breath quickened. Arousal tightened in my core until something inside of me was ready to release at the pleasure of it. But it wasn't my intimate muscles. It was something deeper.

"What's happening?" I asked.

But Zane only shook his head, his eyes as wide with the same confusion as mine.

"Your light wants to touch, but your flesh is in the way."

The connection broke at the sound of another voice hovering above us. Zane yanked his hand from my face. We both turned to see Eden watching us.

There was interest in her impassive gaze. And she wasn't alone. The dragon-riding woman stood next to her.

"I'm told that coupling with your genitals is pleasurable." Eden wrinkled her nose as she said it. "But it pales in comparison to when you intermix your light with another's."

The dragon lady beside Eden peered down at us. Not at us. At Zane. She looked at his package and her face said she was all kinds of impressed.

I had the instinct to screech at her like an angry cat whose territory she was encroaching on. But she didn't even spare me a glance.

"I found my time with your father quite pleasurable," said Eden.

I balked, but the comment was addressed to the dragon lady. The young woman's eyes widened, as did her lips, but it was clearly revulsion on her lips.

"Mother," she groaned. "I do not want to hear that."

Eden only shrugged. "Most creatures like to hear the story of their creation, but not my daughters."

Daughter? This was one of Eden's daughters? I wondered if Eden had made her that uniform. I doubted it with the crap job she'd done on my plain sheath.

"Can I take him home with me, Mother? Please?" Eden's daughter fixed her gaze on Zane's chest.

"No, Bryn."

"What use do you have of a dead warrior?" Bryn whined.

"He's not human or dead. He's an Ishim. And, besides, he's already entwined his soul with Nia."

Bryn pouted like a two-year-old denied candy. At the same time, her eyes sparkled like a grown woman intent on getting what she wanted.

Eden turned her attention back to me and Zane. "Pleasurable as exchanging your essence might be, it is considered impolite to do it out in the open."

She raised her brow at us, and it felt like I'd been caught with my skirt up in the backseat of my boyfriend's car. Her point made, Eden glided away and dissipated into thin air.

"So, you're the one that all the fuss is about." Bryn's golden eyes latched onto me. But only for a second. They quickly gravitated back to Zane. "Personally, I would've chosen the dark, broody one, but I've been known to like a fine French wine every now and then."

What the hell was she talking about? I looked to Zane, but he arched his brows in disinterest, giving her the barest bit of attention.

Bryn winked at Zane, then smirked at me. "Anyway, she's the reason I'm here, Mother."

Bryn turned to look at the empty space Eden had left more than a moment ago. Bryn stomped her foot and rolled her eyes skyward.

"I hate when she does that. Mother!" she called into thin air. "Mother! Wait! I need a word."

"It will have to wait," came Eden's disembodied voice. "Mother has a meeting."

"But Father sent me. It's important."

"I'm busy, Bryn."

"You're always busy."

"Go and have something sweet while I tend to my work. I won't be but an instant."

"An instant to you is easily a year in normal time," whined Bryn.

There was no response.

Bryn clenched her fists and screwed up her face at the empty air. For a split second, I felt sympathy. My dad had done just the same to me, disappeared and left me frustrated and in need.

But Bryn caught my gaze. She squinted her eyes and groaned with irritation, then stormed off in those fine boots to find her mother.

CHAPTER EIGHT

I'd walked hand in hand with Zane for hundreds of years, thousands. He'd touched me in more intimate ways than hand to hand. But now, in this moment, every rub of the pad of his thumb sent a thrill of warmth through me. Every catch of his fingernail made my breath catch.

It was uncanny how it felt like we were strolling around on a warm summer's day. But that wasn't the sky I tilted my face up toward. It was the molten metal of the Earth's core.

It streamed down the face of tall, mountain-like structures. The lava flow was like a light show with strobing reds and oranges. Golden sparks snapped into the air like sparklers. We should've been vaporized, but I felt like I was on the boardwalk at an oceanside resort.

"You haven't told me about how it went with your father," Zane said.

I shrugged, not wanting the emotionless meeting to interfere with the pleasant hum growing between us. Eden had said that exchanging our essence was pleasurable, and she was right.

When Zane's light had touched mine moments ago, it stirred a deep need within. The sensations went beyond the summit point of a sexual climax. They started at the peak and steadily climbed upward.

I could only feel fragments of Zane through my skin now, but my marrow told me there was more. I was eager to get him alone, somewhere secluded, to figure out how intimacy worked in this garden paradise. But while we were still out in the open, where a deeper connection would be impolite, I decided to answer his question about my dad.

"There weren't any tears or hugs or *I love yous*," I said.

What had I expected? For my father to hold his arms open to me? For the man—was he even a man?—to pull me close and tell me he missed me? For a being older than I could even comprehend to say that he was happy to have me home after all this time?

Honestly? Yeah. Yeah, that's what I'd been hoping.

"Same here," said Zane.

I'd almost forgotten he'd met with his father as well. When I'd awakened to Eden knitting me up, she'd said that Zane's father had already come and collected him. "I met your father. Well, I saw him. He didn't introduce himself or pay me any heed actually."

"Yeah, Michael isn't the touchy-feely type either."

"I think he might be the archangel from the Bible. The one who led the army of God against Satan's forces. Only it was dragons and not demons or fallen angels."

I had never put much stock in that collection of religious books. I'd always known there was something off about them. Now that I was down here, where Hell should be, based upon biblical logic, having come face to face with God herself, and having met real live angels who didn't seem at all interested in watching over the shoulders of the downtrodden or underdogs, I felt vindicated in my lack of belief.

"That was the impression I got," said Zane. "He appeared to be quite militaristic."

"You know that the Elohim are meeting right now? They're using our memories to determine whether or not to begin the Apocalypse."

Zane nodded. Then he took in a deep breath and sighed. The sound was not one of optimism.

"Well, we can't just stand here," I said. "We have to do something."

Zane turned to me with a look I knew all too well. It was his *I have to talk you out of one of your harebrained ideas* look. Mixed with his *Can't we just have a good time instead of you picking a fight* look. And a touch of his *I'm about to get punched in the face as I stand beside you and support you in your cray-cray* look.

But then his eyes slipped past me. His gaze narrowed. Something dark moved in the reflection of his pupils. Zane pulled me flush to his body, turning me to the side. He raised his free hand as though to ward off an attack.

I felt the impact strike him and the pain ripple through his body. It wasn't a punch in the face as he stood beside me. It was a flint dagger through the palm.

Anger and menace rolled through Zane. The

feelings then rose through his thin pores as a thin, steamy mist of golden energy. He continued to shield me as I tried to get around him to face the threat. An attack against one of us was an attack against both.

"It should be enough that you've found your way down here so soon," came a dark voice that dripped with false sincerity.

I knew that voice. "Yod?"

"But your death doesn't assuage my need for revenge."

Yod came into view. Unlike Zane, he wasn't naked. He'd cloaked himself in dark fabric that fit his lean body quite well. I felt a prick of betrayal that his outfit was tailored and mine was shaped like a sack.

"You killed me," Yod snarled. His chest was puffed out. His breaths came out in noisy gusts. His teeth were bared.

"I didn't mean to." I raised my hands in placation, but then the memory of that ordeal back in the ruins of Mosul came back to me.

Yod mistaking Loren for Gwin. The dagger at my best friend's throat. Her body falling to the ground. The maroon stain on her chest. Her eyes going lifeless as I held her in my arms.

True, she'd lived. And, yeah, she'd come away

from that deathly experience with a huge boon: magical powers, a new family, an ancient title, and a whole new life. But the major plot point of that story was that she'd died first, and it had been all Yod's fault.

My gaze found Yod's and I dropped all pretense of peace. "You threatened the life of my best friend."

"A human?" His eyes nearly bugged out of his head with incredulity. "You ended my life over a human."

"Loren's a witch, and a knight of the Round Table, actually." I said the words with pride. "Besides, you're still alive and living in paradise."

"Paradise?" Yod roared. "I had an army of nitwit humans up there. I was a god. But down here, I'm nothing. I'm powerless. This is hell."

"So go back," I said.

The anger fell from Yod's face. His fists unballed and his shoulders slumped. In front of me I felt Zane's shoulders tense as though he was preparing to protect me from an unseen threat. Off to the side, Epsilon and Vau were coming closer to us from a path. They stopped and watched the scene go down. Neither of them met my gaze. The silence felt ripe.

"We can go back?" I asked. "To the surface. Can't we?"

When no one responded, I turned to Vau. Her brows drew close together and she looked away from me while placing a thumb to her ear.

"We never asked," she said, rubbing the lobe of her ear. "Epsilon and I haven't wanted to return. There's nothing there for us. Especially if you remember the way we left. Did the Xia really drink our bones?"

I nodded.

Vau let go of her earlobe and looked to Epsilon. A shudder went through her frame, and he pulled her close. The memories from the cave in the Gongyi went through me and I shuddered too.

Warm arms came around me as they had the two times I'd been in that cave in the south of China. Unlike Vau and Epsilon, I'd had a saving grace. Zane had come to my rescue.

"We have no desire to return to the surface," said Epsilon. "We just want to live quietly down here together. We don't have to part down here. There's no sickness, no allergy. No one after us. It's peaceful. This is the true heaven. At least for us."

He looked at Vau with a love so palpable I could feel it shining on my skin. Yod turned his back on them in disgust. Zane remained by my side in quiet support.

"You've been digging all of your life, Theta," said Vau. They were the same words Eden had said to me. "I think it might've been an attempt to come back here. All the answers to questions you never even thought to ask are down here. You can be with Zane. He can paint and sculpt. You don't have to leave each other, because you won't get weak or weary in this thin skin."

She had a point. I was itching to get back into Eden's lab. I wanted a closer look at her writings, and I wanted to know more about that nuclear globe she'd stopped me from touching.

And there were materials and colors in this garden that Zane had yet to experiment with. There was also that added bit about the lack of allergic reactions. It did seem like paradise. But...

"I can't stand by and let a whole race of beings be wiped out of existence," I said.

"Might be the best thing for us all if that's the verdict," said Epsilon.

I turned on him, my gaze mutinous. But Vau had his back.

"Humans have spread over the earth like a disease, over land and seas. The oceans cover three quarters of this planet. Yet humans pump the core for oil. They spill their toxic waste. The way that the climate has changed and the planet has warmed is affecting the seas. Some of their unnatural plastics have even made their way down here into the core."

Vau had always loved the seas. We'd traveled them together back when she was alive. She was never far from water.

"In the time I've been away," she continued, "they've polluted the sky. Nature is turning against them, giving them cancers, making them barren, leeching the sanity from their minds. And still they haven't learned. I don't believe they will. I've already died once because of them. I don't want to do it again. And at the rate they're going, the whole planet is in danger."

CHAPTER NINE

There were dwellings in this place. But they didn't look like homes. I couldn't quite determine what material they were made of. Some looked to be made of rock, others of crystal, and others looked mossy, like vegetation.

Many of the buildings had no roofs. There were seating areas, but otherwise they were open and airy, like they were built for beings who flew and who preferred the natural state of light, which could penetrate most things. Therefore why would doors even be necessary?

A few places looked like what we'd call homes on the surface. I knew Vau's home the moment I laid eyes on it. It was shaped like a pyramid mound. Vau and I had spent a lot of time in Egypt. Her final earthly home had been a pyramid mound in the Gongyi territory of China. This was a near-exact replica.

Even though we'd just had it out, she welcomed me into her home. Of course she did. She was my oldest friend, my sister.

Yod had taken off the moment Vau and I had started our disagreement. Typical. The bastard thrived on discord and was happy when he'd sown it.

But he was wrong. Vau and I had had many disagreements in the past. We knew how to fight and still care for each other. She reached for me and brought me into her arms.

I tensed, but this time, instead of seeing her death, she showed me snippets of our adventures together. The two of us sailing the Mediterranean. Buying silks in India. Laughing and dancing as Zane and Epsilon watched us in the light of a fire.

They were happy memories. Ones I cherished. But they weren't what was on my mind. My energy focused on all the stories I'd captured, the ones I was still figuring out, and the ones that would never be told if the vote went against humanity.

"You're exactly like her," said Vau when she

pulled away from me. "Eden saves everything that has ever lived."

"Now she's going to purposely eradicate a whole species," I said.

"It wouldn't be the first time. It won't be the last."

"It's not right," I insisted. "It's not fair."

"Maybe not," said Vau. "But it is balance. We live at the core of a spinning orb. If it goes out of balance, we all perish. You'll come to see she's right. Not now, but maybe in a few centuries or a millennium. Then you'll get to be a part of something new. You can record from the beginning."

People kept saying that, but they were wrong. It was the past that interested me most. Vau left the room, shutting the door behind her. When she was gone, I turned to Zane.

He stood by silently, leaning against a wall in the recesses of the room that would be ours in Vau and Epsilon's home. There were only the four walls and a mossy bed tucked into the corner of the room. Zane looked tired. And as if to punctuate the point, he sighed, his shoulders drooping in defeat.

Without a word, he kicked off the wall. He took a few steps for the doorway. My heart sank to think I'd lost his support too.

"You side with her?" I asked.

Zane opened his mouth to speak—

"Don't tell me you have issues with humans too? What have they ever done to you?"

"You're looking for a fight," he said. "But I'm not going to give it to you."

I stood in his path and stared at him. Anger pinched the tips of my fingers. But I opened my hands and let it go.

Zane and I knew how to fight too. We weren't the type of couple that needed to agree on everything. We could disagree. Eventually, he'd see he was wrong, and I was right.

"I'm sorry," I offered.

"I know," he conceded.

"I love you," I tried.

"I know," he conceited.

I huffed in exasperation. Infuriating man.

Zane's lips quirked up in amusement. He leaned down and kissed my shoulders. Then he kissed the side of my neck.

The pressure of his soft lips left scorch marks on my skin. Energy stirred in the core of my soul, building like a hurricane. But I stepped out of the storm and gathered my wits in the calm of the eye.

"I'm going to go talk to Eden," I said.

"I knew that, too." Zane sighed. Then he let go of

me. "I was so much better at this seduction stuff above ground."

"You are perfect." I placed my hand on his strong jaw. "You are sexy and desirable, and I would totally be jumping your bones and trying to figure out how to peel back your skin to get to your energy. But the fate of the world is on the line."

"It always is with you, Nova."

"This isn't about me," I protested.

"Of course it is," he said. "It always has been. You want to save the world and now you have the perfect platform and your greatest adversary. A freaking god, Nova. Not *a* god, *the* god."

Zane shook his head and turned, preparing to cross the threshold.

"Where are you going?"

"To find a pair of pants," he said. "If we're going to fight an ethereal god, I should do it wearing pants."

The storm died around me. The sun rose, and in the face of that brilliant star, I saw the face of this man that I loved with every lumen inside me. His light surrounded me, never letting cold reality pierce me too deeply.

"But you don't agree with me," I said.

"It's not the first time. It won't be the last."

"You're not abandoning me?"

"Why would you think that?" He turned back to me, his brows nearing his hairline in incredulity. "You may be a self-centered demigod who thinks the world revolves around her."

I waited for the positive spin on those cutting words. And waited. "Your point being?"

He shrugged. "My point being that, for me, it's always about you."

My features softened. My insides softened. "You're going to stand by me in this crazy fight?"

"I am crazy in love with you, aren't I? Besides, the last time I stood by you, you got me killed. What more could possibly go wrong?"

I brushed that stubborn lock of hair out of his face. But the lock fell back over his eyes. It had always been this way. This lock of hair had been stubborn for as long as I'd known Zane, and he put up with it.

He preferred to keep his hair long, and I'd known this lock as long as I'd known him. It seemed to want attention, and would stand front and center whenever it got the chance. He simply put up with it because it was a part of him.

I pressed my lips to the lock. It fell away, parting

until my lips met warm flesh. The heat of his internal light greeted my lips.

Zane's eyes fluttered closed. He let out a soft moan. I entwined my fingers with his. He needed to know that I was here for him too, that I would always be here for him. He opened his eyes and stared at me.

"How are you feeling?" I asked, cradling his palm. He'd pulled out the shank Yod had thrown, but his skin hadn't reknitted.

"Like a piece of me has been ripped apart." He shrugged. "I've felt worse. I've had my heart broken."

"I'm sorry. I keep putting you in harm's way."

"I know what I signed up for," he said. "If Tres could see me now. Doubt he'd trade places."

"I don't want someone to hurt you to get to me. And I never want you to hurt again, for any reason."

My eyes burned. Tears pooled at the corners. I was surprised there was any liquid inside of me since I hadn't eaten or drank anything since my rebirth.

"Hey, come here," said Zane.

I took a deep breath in and sighed. My struggle was only a pretense. I came into his arms. His skin was so thin, the heat of his light seeped into mine.

I inched my fingers down along his until our

digits met at the webbing between each finger. When we touched, memories swirled from my chest because, I realized, that's where most of my memories of Zane were stored.

I pushed that energy to the forefront. I wanted him to see those memories, to drown in those feelings. He breathed a sigh deeper than mine.

It felt like relief. It felt like gratitude. It felt like love.

I tilted my head back and met his lips. I'd kissed this man for centuries, but with the truth of who we both were so close to the surface, it was like we kissed for the first time.

Heat rushed to my lips. My lips immediately swelled, as though all the energy in my body rushed to that spot, hoping for a taste of him. I reached out and clung to his shoulders, needing his strength to steady me.

But the added contact of my palms against his bare skin only pulled the energy from my head to my hands and left me even more lightheaded. My toes tingled, so light from the loss of energy I thought I'd float away. I anchored my hands around Zane and pulled him closer, and even closer, needing desperately to shake loose this cumbersome flesh to get to the heart of him.

I scratched at my chest. My nail snagged at the skin covering my heart, and the thin veil of flesh tore. Light trickled out.

Zane pulled back, his eyes wide. "Are you sure?"

"For better or worse," I said.

I was now certain we breathed air and our lungs did, in fact, need it to survive beneath the surface. I was certain that we were alive and not dead. My breath caught in my throat and my heart sank into my gut like I had just died.

My fingers trembled as I reached out to him. When my skin met his, I saw a montage of my face. Really it was mostly my lips.

My lips split in a smile. My lips rounded in an O of surprise. My lips widened as passion was wrenched from me.

I stepped into Zane. Fell into him, and he caught me. Like he always did. When I was at my best or my worst, he was always there. When I'd loved him well, when I'd behaved badly, even if his back was turned, he always reached for me. I'd never once fallen without his arms, his heart, his love as a soft cushion.

"Kiss me," I said, my voice desperate.

He grinned, the devil in the glint of his eyes. "Where?"

"My soul."

He kissed me on my chest, at the space where I'd torn my skin. He poured into me as his breaths mingled and mixed with my essence. I felt myself bursting forth. The true me burned against the skin that covered my light and the thing that I was made of poured out. Zane's soul poured into me.

We tumbled onto the mossy bed. My head bounced from the impact.

"That's one way to try to take my head off," I said.

"I'm so sorry, *mon coeur*." But he chuckled as he said it.

I reversed our positions and mounted him. He was already naked, at least his body was. I grabbed for the edges of the sheath I wore and tugged it up. He didn't help me. He simply watched.

Zane's fingers traced my rib cage. Then he cupped my breasts. His thumbs rubbed at my nipples, drawing them into taut points. All his attention focused as he handled my right breast.

"What?" I asked. "Did Eden get something wrong?"

He frowned. "I think she may have changed your cup size."

I threw the balled-up sheath at his head. "Jerk."

He chuckled again, and then tossed me on my

back. But he didn't take the upper hand. He laid me down so that we were side by side. His face turned serious.

"Forgive me," he said, his features suddenly grave.

"What sin have you committed?"

He swallowed before he answered. "I doubted you. I doubted what has always been between us."

I shook my head, taking his hand in mine and joining us down to the webbing once more. "You had every right. I let the memories slip through my fingers."

"I should've never let you get too far away from me."

"Zane, I don't want to do this."

He pulled back. His warm skin leaving mine left me cold. I reached for him before he could get any farther.

"I don't want to assign blame or give forgiveness," I said. "I just want to be. I just want to be with you. Can we just be?"

He smiled and pressed his lips to mine. No blame. No forgiveness. Not even any gratitude.

His kiss was life as it should be. Me and Zane. Zane and I. Together.

Need grew in my belly as our torsos pressed

together. I couldn't get close enough to him. Damn this skin. It felt suffocating. I needed to get it off so that I could consume him.

I scratched at my chest, needing him closer. My skin tore a bit more and it was such a relief it felt like an orgasm. Zane bent his head down to touch my light with his lips again. Any climax I'd had in the past three thousand years had not been anything like loving in the light.

The light in the room was glaringly bright. It crawled up the back of my spine and made me tense. It felt off. It felt different. Familiar but foreign. Like something else was in the room. I looked up, and Gabriel, my father, stood in the open doorway. He watched us impassively.

I yelped and grabbed for my sheath. Zane stood, shielding me, and faced my father.

"With all due respect," Zane said through clenched teeth, "you could announce yourself before coming into a room."

Gabriel cocked his head to the side like a confused bird. "I stood in the doorway and flashed my light."

Zane looked to me. I looked to him. Then we both turned back to gape at my father.

"Your presence is needed at the gathering."

Gabriel turned and headed out, likely expecting us to follow his command.

With the sheath covering my body, I looked again to Zane. He pinched the bridge of his nose. I smoothed the sheath down and my hand froze.

"Wait," I yelled. "Gabriel?"

My father rematerialized in the doorway in an instant, his expression blank.

"Um… could you… would you mind?" I shifted the sheath and pointed to my chest where the torn light was coming through.

I was mortified. What daughter in the history of the world had to get her father to stitch up her skin after amorous activity? Anybody else? No? It was just my luck.

CHAPTER TEN

I slipped on the discarded sheath and squirmed as Gabriel stitched up my skin. Zane stood off to the side. His gaze was a narrow slit of irritation, but his lips twitched in amusement as he watched the man who had sired me reknit the skin on my chest, which had been torn due to my haste to jump his bones.

As my father's light connected with mine, it brought a different heat than Zane's. Gabriel's light was familiar, but it ran a bit cold. I studied the details of my sire's face. Had he ever looked on me warmly? I couldn't recall a single instance.

Once Gabriel was done, he backed away. He tilted his head, signaling for me to precede him out the door. Zane brought up the rear.

"Eden only asked for her," said Gabriel.

"Where she goes, I follow," said Zane.

"Yes," said Gabriel. "I remember that about you two."

We left the pyramid and headed outside. It was perpetual day here in the core. Light everywhere. Light above, light below, light emanating off the beings walking and floating around.

"Gabriel? Has a decision been made? Are the Elohim waging war against humanity?"

"Elohim do not wage war," he said. "We keep the balance. Humans have tilted the scales too far. Things must be righted."

"Like with the dragons?"

"Exactly."

"But you didn't just wipe out the dragons. You wiped out most of the creatures who roamed on the surface at that time. Didn't that create another imbalance?"

"Yes, at the time." Gabriel nodded. "But in the end, all was righted and brought back into balance. If it had not been, we could've all perished. Dragons evolved to breathe fire. Humans have learned to create bombs. The bombs would devastate more of life than a stream of fire from a single dragon."

I couldn't argue that. And when I remained mute

and stewing, Gabriel turned back around and continued on. I looked at Zane, but he had no words to offer. So we fell into step behind Gabriel.

We returned to the structure where I'd awakened. This time, the heat inside overwhelmed me. It was like a sauna, but it felt good on my skin, like I'd stepped into the summer sun after having been lost in centuries of winter.

Elohim were everywhere. Dozens of them. It was difficult to tell many of the Elohim's gender. Sex wasn't a natural trait for beings who started as specks of light encased in membranes.

None had hair. Instead, only a pattern of raised nodes swirled around the crowns of their heads. Many of them sat in their natural light. The few who had skin favored the tones on the darker side of the spectrum. None wore clothes.

I saw the Trickster Twins, Hunahpú and Xbalanqué. I ached to go to them and ask them of Skye and Skully. They'd just left their children, the Balam and the Mohegan shifters, before Zane and I had fallen to the core. The shifters would surely be on their fathers' minds.

It hadn't quite been a twenty-four-hour day since Zane and I had fallen through the door. Had it? How long since the Twins had shut the door. How long had they stayed on the surface? How long had we been down here?

I started to make my way over toward them, certain that Zane was at my back. But when I looked over my shoulder, Zane stood stock still. His gaze narrowed at the center of the room.

There was one Elohim on the floor. Though his speech was emotionless and his features impassive, his words were filled with fire and brimstone.

"We feel the irritation of the Earth," said Michael. "The answer is clear. Something must be done on the surface before the scourge of humanity infects the core."

A memory of a place flitted to the surface of my consciousness. Somewhere situated off the west coast of Turkey and the continent of Asia. Patmos, I believe it was called. It wasn't even the turn of the millennium. There I looked over the shoulder of a man as he wrote a book using similar fiery language.

"The nations were angry, and your wrath has come," said that man on that island. "The time has come for judging the dead, and for rewarding your servants the prophets and your people who revere your name, both great and small, and for destroying those who destroy the earth."

John had been his name. He was an older man,

and many called him John the Elder. John the Elder went on to write a book. *Revelations,* he'd called it.

John had stood in the middle of the streets most days shouting about the end of days. "And the kings of the earth, the great men, the rich men, the commanders, the mighty men, every slave and every free man, hid themselves in the caves and in the rocks of the mountains, and said to the mountains and rocks, 'Fall on us and hide us from the face of Him who sits on the throne and from the wrath of the Lamb! For the great day of His wrath has come, and who is able to stand?'"

John once said he'd heard the trumpets of the angels and seen a fiery light. I wondered if Michael had paid him a vision.

Out in the hall, many of the Elohim nodded in agreement with Michael. But there was at least one voice of dissent.

"We've felt this disturbance before, with the fae," said another Elohim. A woman. I recognized her. It was Rhea, the mother of the Olympian gods.

She had come to me in my dreams not long ago. She'd asked me to help save her children, the Greek gods. Perhaps she might be an ally now, especially since her children were still above on the surface and humans were their livelihood.

"Yes, but at least the fae had the wherewithal to remove themselves," said Michael. "Humanity doesn't possess the intellect to do so. They do possess the intellect to manipulate energy. Their bombs could destroy us all."

"My children are still up there," said Rhea.

Michael shrugged. "So are some of mine. I fail to see your point."

Beside me, Zane tensed at his father's words. I wrapped my hand around his bicep. Zane wouldn't do anything, I didn't think. I just needed him to know that I was with him.

"Hello, little Ishim."

It was Eden's daughter, Bryn. She leaned against the frame of the door, half in and half out. She tilted her head to the side in that curious way that her mother did. But her gaze was shrewd, calculating.

"You don't know who I am? Do you?" she asked.

"Sure I do," I said. "You're Eden's brat."

Bryn's shrewd calculations came to a sum. "Poor little Ishim and their tiny brains." Her gaze slipped past me and perused Zane.

I wasn't a possessive woman. Not really. But something about this chick rankled me. "Keep your dim little fingers off my man, or else."

"Or else what?" She smirked.

I reached down to my thigh only to remember I had no blades. Meanwhile, Bryn held a sword at her back. How come I didn't get any steel?

"Bryn, play nice." Eden's voice was unmistakable.

Even without recognizing her voice, I felt her light. It was like no other light in existence. Strong as a heartbeat that pulsed through you.

"Why?" Bryn's voice was little more than a throaty whine. "She's just an Ishim."

"So are you."

"I'm the daughter of two ethereal beings. Not some bloody human." Bryn pouted and stomped her boot on the ground.

"Mother has work to do," said Eden. "Go and play with the flora while I talk to Nia."

"I'm your daughter." Bryn balled her fingers into fists. "You've been putting me off all day when I have something important to tell you."

"You're being dramatic. It's a flaw in my daughters' design." Eden looked at Bryn, cocking her head from side to side in that curious expression. "I think perhaps too much light. Bryn, I'm sure whatever you have to say to me can wait a bit longer."

"I won't bother to wait. I'll return home to Asgard since you don't have time for me."

Asgard? That place wasn't real. The realm of Odin and the Valkyrie.

But then I took Bryn in again. The fae ears. The soldier's outfit. The sword. Valkyrie rode horses, sometimes unicorns. But honestly, was a fire-breathing dragon that far off from a unicorn? She was a freaking Valkyrie.

"I'll just return to Father then," said Bryn as she turned. "I only came to tell you about the theft of the Hammer of God."

Eden's head jerked back. "Someone stole Odin's hammer?"

"Hmm," sing-songed Bryn, still heading away but walking extremely slowly. "A witch."

That perked up my ears. A witch? A thief? Facing off against a god? Could it be?

"You've always had a fondness for telling stories, Bryn," said Eden. "I'm busy now. I'll give you my attention when I'm finished. Why don't you go and play with Zayin while I speak with Nia?"

Eden beckoned to me. I hesitated, looking between the Creator, her demon offspring, and my soulmate. Bryn's pretend steps toward her home halted, and she turned back and grinned at Zane. Zane raised a wary eyebrow at Bryn and then winked at me. He could handle her, the wink said. I sighed and reluctantly followed Eden.

"Your daughter is a spoiled brat," I said to Eden while we were still within earshot.

"No." Eden frowned. "I don't think so. From my understanding, a spoiled brat is a child who uses their parents' weaknesses to get what they want. I don't have any weaknesses."

She had a point there. Not about the weaknesses, about Bryn getting what she wanted. Bryn was clearly not getting what she wanted from her mother, which was attention. Put like that, I had a momentary pang for the girl. But only a tiny pang. She was still a holy terror.

"And I only brought them into existence," Eden was saying. "They were raised by their father."

"Odin? He's in Asgard? Where is that?"

"Another realm inside the earth."

"There are other realms?"

"You're standing in the core right now. This is a big planet. Lots of nooks and crannies to exist within."

We arrived back in Eden's lab, tidy as ever, the exam table bare. Did she only use it to knit back fallen Ishim, or did she experiment on the various life forms of creation? I wasn't sure I wanted to know.

"I developed those symbols because I needed a way to communicate with others." Eden's slender fingers waved at the bright graffiti of pictographs that hung in the air, much like Zane's painting. "Elohim communicated with our light. Then mouths evolved and we began making sounds. Did you know that the first sound was El?"

Having only been born three thousand years ago, I did not know that fun fact.

"I developed taste to guide life forms into understanding dangers of certain elements. With noses I established scent. With the eyes came writings. But, at the end of the cycle, all communication is light."

"Why are you telling me this?" I asked.

"You're a good storyteller. I like the way you've catalogued your memories and humanity's stories. I'd like for you to work with me."

"Work with you?"

"Keeping the records of existence."

I opened my mouth, but then closed it. Most of my records were of those cultures and civilizations that had been wiped out due to genocide and war and strife. I wrote down the stories of the marginalized, those who were covered up and buried in the dirt. What Eden was offering me now was a dream job.

"You've decided to save humanity?" I asked.

"Oh. No. The pattern of the human race's destructive nature is strong. They need to go."

My throat went dry. Like a brittle, cold day with a raspy wind that blew away a scarf.

"But not all," Eden clarified. "I'll save a few humans for the records. You can even pick a few hundred of your favorites, if you'd like."

"Save a few humans? Like in Noah's Ark?"

"Who?" She frowned. "Humans have lost their connection. All other animals still heed the rules of nature. But humanity goes against it. My hands are tied. Is that how the phrase goes?"

"That's not true," I said, and then groped for evidence. I hadn't been able to make a valid argument to Vau or Epsilon, or to my father. I'd had these thoughts myself from time to time.

"Humans are connected," I said. "By the blood in their veins. They protect each other, even as they fight each other. That's admirable. Just because they haven't served your purpose doesn't mean they're bad. They love hard, create beauty, solve problems in new and interesting ways."

True, their love easily turned to hate. Yeah, they often destroyed the beauty they created. And maybe they were often behind the problems that needed solving.

"I like you," said Eden with a nod of approval. "You have fire in your belly. Like a dragon. They were one of my favorite life forms."

Hope sprung up in my heart. She was feeling nostalgic. She had said she'd hated destroying the dragons. Maybe she was having second thoughts about humans.

"So, you've changed your mind?" I asked.

"No, I believe it's time."

"Time for what?"

"The apocalypse."

My heart sank to my bare feet and my legs shook. No, that wasn't me shaking. The ground shook.

CHAPTER ELEVEN

*B*OOM!

I'd been in an earthquake before. During that natural disaster, the first indication was a bump, like rolling over a speed hump at low speed in a vehicle. Several seconds later was the telltale shaking of the ground. That sharp shake caused buildings to rattle, glass to break, and brick to fall. But it all passed relatively quickly.

This was no typical earthquake. The earth below and the faux sky above rattled like a beast trying to escape a cage. The shocking vibrations weren't quick or fleeting. The shivering of the earth lasted for long moments. Waves of energy passed through me, like a strong wind. But it didn't knock me down.

It had started. The apocalypse. There was nothing I could do.

Everyone above that I loved was gone or suffering. I wanted to punch something, preferably Eden. But the look on her face left my fingers numb.

The blast hadn't knocked Eden down, but it did knock the impassivity off her face. I didn't know true fear until I saw the face of God contorted in shock and uncertainty. Whatever had exploded, whatever had been destroyed, whatever was coming, it wasn't by her design.

"Huh," she said, cocking her head in that birdlike fashion. "That is new."

Then her face took on a dreamy look.

"It has been so long since I've had a new experience."

I didn't wait around for Eden to revel in the moment. I hurried out of the lab. The Elohim spilled out of the hall. I expected them to surround Eden, to protect her. But none of them even approached her. I supposed that made sense since she was more powerful than all of them. They could do nothing to protect her.

Gabriel searched the crowd until he found me. Was that relief or accusation on his face? I wasn't sure.

Michael stood at the perimeter. Sword of light raised, looking for a battle.

"What was that?" someone asked.

Eden looked around. I knew she wasn't looking with her eyes, but with her inner light. Confusion remained on her face. For once, she didn't know something.

The shaking stopped. But the vibration of the disturbance remained. And then a voice sounded in the silence.

"Kneeee-ahhh."

A throaty voice, like a smoker. The consonants came off the tongue clipped and harsh like she was South African. But there was an added softening to the end of my name, lengthening the vowel sound as though the speaker had leisure time at her hands and the freedom to spend it.

"Dr. Nia Rivers."

The voice that bellowed my name was deep. But it was also high-pitched and feminine. I was hallucinating. I had to be. It simply wasn't possible.

"Girl, you better get your hot ass out here. And bring that fine Frenchman with you. Your ride is here."

Loren? Loren. "Loren!"

Zane drew close behind me. His was the only

face not contorted in confusion. His lips quirked in amusement.

Beside him, Bryn had her hand cocked on her hip. "Told you," she told her mother. "I tried to tell you someone was coming for her. But you didn't have time to listen."

Dozens of bright eyes shifted from Bryn to me. I had to assume break-ins and rescue attempts weren't a common occurrence in the core of the Earth. There was likely no protocol for what was happening. Instead of waiting around for them to figure out what action to take, I grabbed Zane and took off.

We ran out of the bright hall into the cool warmth of the outside. And there she was, like a blonde, avenging angel.

"What the hell?" I said. "How the hell?"

Loren grinned. She was dressed in a simple T-shirt and jeans. She looked rumpled and worn, but still a glorious, welcome sight. Instead of her usual blade, she swung a metallic hammer in her hand.

"I was led to believe this wasn't hell," Loren said, "but some kind of angel spa? And you didn't invite me."

She pouted at me. I flew into her arms. Holding her to me. Testing her realness.

It was her. She was here and real and alive.

She was solid and flesh and fine material, like she'd been the last time I'd seen her. But she was stronger than the last time, when she'd been on her deathbed. She was tanned and muscled and here.

"How is this even possible?" I asked, still unable, unwilling, to let her go.

Loren shrugged one shoulder, looking not in the least bit contrite. "I may have borrowed the hammer of a god that allows me to break through the nine realms of the earth."

"Borrowed?" I pulled away and eyed her suspiciously.

Loren clucked her tongue. "Are we seriously going to argue about how I got the getaway car?"

"Ladies, this reunion is great, but we should start the engines."

Beyond Loren, Tres stood backlit by the lava flow coming down one of the volcanic mountains of the core. His brown skin, tinted copper, cast a shade over him that made him look like a god. His brow was quirked in that expectant way of his, that way that said he'd have his way and you would like it. His tone brooked no argument that his edict would not be followed.

I didn't do as he said. I never did. I never had.

I'm sure he expected my rebellion because, when I flew into his arms, he held onto me for a moment instead of steering me where he wanted me to go.

"You came," I said.

"Of course I did."

He smelled so familiar: the musk of frankincense, the salty sweat of the earth, and the spice that was uniquely Tres. It had only been a day since I'd last left him, weeks since we'd been lovers, centuries since we'd been friends, but I'd missed him.

As I stood in his embrace, memories flooded to the front of my mind. Just as Zane was always near me, Tres was never far from his best friend. I didn't doubt that Tres had feelings for me, but those feelings had never once come close to what he felt for Zane. Which was why Tres's feelings for me had caused him to suffer so in his life.

Tres was in the skin he'd been born with, so his light wasn't in direct contact with mine, which meant I didn't know what he was thinking in the moment or in the past. But I still felt him. Holding him, I didn't feel the suffering over his illicit feelings any longer. Just relief.

And then he stiffened.

Tres looked behind me. I knew who was there without turning, but I turned nonetheless.

Zane and Tres faced off. Silently for a moment. I wanted to echo Tres's edict to get a move on, to jump in the getaway car and out of this place.

Even now Elohim surrounded us. Moving in quickly and quietly. But I couldn't interrupt this moment for the two men.

Tres reached out his hand to Zane. Zane looked down at it. Zane took one step, then another, and then embraced Tres.

Tres sighed, heavily enough for the stream of air to jostle my sheath. The weight of hundreds of years fell off his shoulders and left his heart. And then a dark shadow broke the moment.

"You're just in time, son," said Michael.

Tres stepped out of Zane's embrace. Both men's dark gazes alighted on Michael. Zane held his brother's forearm. I wasn't sure if it was to hold Tres back or to offer him support for this big reveal.

"Son?" Tres looked Michael up and down.

Tres hadn't come here the normal way, by death. He was fully intact with the same thick skin he'd left this garden with originally. But still, by the look on his face, I felt certain the memories of Michael were rising to the forefront of his crowded mind.

Tres's features contorted with doubt as he took in his father. Like with Zane, there was no resemblance. But I knew Tres could feel the likeness in their shared light.

"Now we see that six Ishim have been cast down by humans," said Michael, his gaze landing on Loren. "I need no more evidence. We need to get on with it."

Michael turned toward Eden, who watched the exchange between the four of us with interest.

"What's he talking about?" asked Loren.

"You interrupted the apocalypse," I said. "They were just debating whether or not to wipe humanity off the surface of the planet."

"What?" said Loren. "Like hell. My family's up there."

"You can perish with the rest of your kind," said Michael. His lip curled.

It was the first bit of emotion I'd ever seen on his face. Behind him, Gabriel remained stoic. Eden looked entertained, like a play she'd written was taking on a life of its own as the actors improvised.

"Are you talking to me?" said Loren. "'Cause you don't know who I am."

I groaned as Loren began an impersonation of a psychotic taxi driver from the movies. Now was not the time. This place, which had no notion of media, was definitely not the right venue.

"I've brought gods to their knees," she continued. "You need to ask somebody, Mr. Glow Stick."

Then her gaze raked over the crowd and her eyes lit.

"In fact, ask him." Loren pointed to Cronus, who stood beside his long-suffering wife Rhea. "Help him to recognize."

"I recognize that you smell delicious," said Cronus. He stepped forward, angling to get closer to Loren, who was half human, but Rhea held him back.

"All right," said Loren. "Everyone who needs a lift up top, grab onto the blonde witch."

She swung the hammer round and round, but on the third go around it flew off her wrist and into Eden's palm. Loren turned to face Eden, stepping into a fighting stance. I wrapped my hand around my best friend's forearm and held her still.

"That's not *a* god," I said. "That's *the* god."

"That's a woman."

I nodded.

"So, God doesn't have balls?" said Loren. "I think we may have finally met our match."

Eden laughed. "I like her. She has spunk. Is that the right word?"

Eden looked over her shoulder at Bryn for confirmation. But Bryn was too busy sneering at Loren.

"You again," said Bryn.

"Hey there, Brian," said Loren.

"You two have met?" said Eden.

Bryn sighed. "I already told you, Mother. She came to Asgard and stole Father's hammer."

"I didn't steal it," Loren insisted. "I borrowed it."

"And she opened the doors to Valhalla, letting loose a horde of our army."

"Yeah," said Loren. "That was my bad. Really sorry about that."

"Oh, you will be sorry." Bryn took a menacing step forward.

Eden stuck her hand out to stay her daughter. "No, no. I'm going to keep this human."

Bryn's smirk fell, and her eyes blazed at her mother.

"I'm no one's pet," said Loren.

"Oh but you'll have your own domicile," said Eden, "decadent foods, servants."

"Wait." Loren cocked her head to the side. "What kinds of foods?"

"Loren," I hissed.

"What? I'm just asking a clarifying question."

"Here." Eden handed Bryn the hammer. "Take this back to your father. Tell him to mind it better."

"But Mother—"

"Run along now, Bryn. Mother has to get back to work."

Bryn's pretty face looked as though someone with big fingers had pinched her features together. Once again, she stomped her foot. She yanked the hammer out of her mother's hand and stormed off.

CHAPTER TWELVE

We were shoved unceremoniously into a dim room with four walls. But they weren't exactly walls. On one side, the boundary was web-like strands, golden and woven like the intricate workings of a spider's web. Getting close to them, I felt the heat radiating from them.

On the other side of the energy web, a lush forest of green treetops reached up to the faux sky. Down below were the colorful vines and fronds of a jungle. The view was beautiful, literally breathtaking.

Two of the opposing walls were earthen stone, but cool to the touch. The fourth wall was the same curtain of shadow that led in and out of Eden's lab. Only this time, when I reached out and touched it, it was solid.

"We've all been held captive before," said Loren. "But you have to admit, this is the nicest place we've ever been trapped in."

The interior was just as lush and dazzling. There was an assortment of seating areas made of wood. But the wood wasn't taken from the ground; it was still rooted into the ground. Moss of different colors acted as cushions to the arboresque appendages. A shelving unit made of branches crawled up the wall. Precious stones and plants rested on the limbs.

Loren was right. This place beat the cold underground cave in the Gongyi when we met in search of dragon bones. It was definitely a prettier sight than the ruins of Eleusis when we faced off against a rising Titan. It was far more peaceful than the mortar and shells raining down over Mosul as we searched for the Holy Grail.

"It's still a cage," said Tres.

"A gilded cage," said Loren. She ran her hand over the knickknacks on the shelving units. I expected her fingers to come away sticky and for something to go missing. But all items on the shelves were still there after Loren removed her hand.

"Only you would care about the decor of your jail," Tres said.

Loren grinned at him, waggling her eyebrows.

She turned her attention to the solid door of light, but not before tossing Tres a wink over her shoulder as she turned.

Tres's look of stoicism slipped. He let out a sigh as he rolled his eyes skyward. The sound wasn't one of annoyance. It was part resignation, part amusement, with a touch of indulgence.

I knew that sound well. It was how he'd reacted to my shenanigans when we were on the road to mending our fractured and forgotten love affair. Tres's eye rolling at Loren ended its circuitous path on me. His throat worked, as though he were gulping down something he had no business consuming. His chin dipped low as if to cover the evidence.

"We wanna escape this beautiful jail," said Loren as she eyed the door. "Okay, let's brainstorm. Maybe I can open a ley line. This place is pure energy."

"No." Tres shook his head vehemently. "I'm not going into another one of your magic holes anytime soon."

"Though out of context, that was deliciously dirty," Loren purred.

Once again Tres rolled his eyes. But this time he made sure not to look my way at the other end.

"Exactly what have you two been up to during your rescue mission?" I asked.

"We traveled through the Bermuda Triangle, which happens to be a passageway into the realm of Asgard," said Loren.

"Asgard?" I asked. There it was again. I supposed that's where she met the lovely Valkyrie, Bryn. "Did you meet Loki and Thor too?"

Tres groaned.

Loren grinned. "They're both very much real, that I can tell you. Oh and I kinda got engaged."

My head jerked to Loren. "Engaged?"

"She's not engaged," growled Tres.

My head whipped to Tres.

"I'm thinking about it," said Loren.

"You can't be serious," said Tres. "He's a lunatic."

"Which one?" I asked. "Who is the lunatic you're thinking about getting engaged to?"

Tres and Loren ignored me and glared at each other, a silent showdown of wills. And then they were not so silent, launching into what appeared to be an argument already in progress. Zane came to stand beside me. His head went left and right from one side of the court to the other as Loren and Tres swung their invectives back and forth.

"You know," said Loren. "For all your bad boy image, you're such a baby."

"You're insane," growled Tres.

Loren shrugged and mouthed *Duh*.

Zane had trouble hiding his smirk as he watched the two.

"You two are awful chummy after spending only a day together," I said.

"You two have been down here for weeks," said Loren.

Weeks? It had barely been twenty-four hours. Though I had yet to see a clock, or anything that kept time. It certainly didn't feel like a full day. With all that had happened, I didn't feel in the least bit tired.

"It's been nearly a month," Loren continued.

"We've been to the ends of the Earth trying to find a way to get down here to you two," said Tres.

Zane looked just as perplexed as I felt. Weeks? Nearly a month? Maybe it was as long as they said. Perhaps time moved differently in the core of the earth.

And now, here they were. Here all of us were. Trapped thousands of miles in the center of the earth.

They'd followed me on another one of my

adventures, and we'd wound up trapped. Tres, Zane, and I wouldn't die. But what about Loren? Though she now had a witch's powers, she was still permanently breakable. It was the Gongyi, Eleusis, Mosul all over again.

"I've put you in danger again," I said to her. "Like always."

"Isn't that what friendship and family is all about?" she said. "Saving each other's ass when we do something stupid. Like die."

Loren balled her fist and hit me in the boob.

"Ow." I doubled over. "What the hell, Loren?"

She'd grown stronger now that she had powers. That actually hurt. I wasn't sure if it was because my skin was so thin, or she was stronger.

"I still don't forgive you for that," she said.

"For what?" I cradled my sore boob in my hand.

"Dying," she shouted. "Do you have any idea what I've been through while you've been dead?" She huffed, reminding me of Bryn. Then she reached to my face. "But damn if it hasn't done wonders for your skin."

Now I grinned. "It's all new flesh."

"What? Is that like some underworld brand of face cream?"

"No. When I fell, it apparently ripped up my

whole body. When I woke up, Eden, that's God's name, was knitting me a whole new body."

"Shut. Up." Loren reached out and touched my neck, my chin, my cheek with her other hand until she cradled my face. "It's as smooth as a baby's bum."

"They're both insane," said Tres. "Stark raving mad."

"You say that like it's your first day," said Zane as he regarded me and Loren with wizened understanding.

Tres glared at his brother. "No, I'm quite used to this. It feels like it's been an eternity, but it's the same story. Me swooping in to save your ass."

Zane scrunched up his nose, smelling something foul. "Let's not forget the reason my ass is in this situation is entirely your fault, which is a story that has been on repeat since we took our first steps on Earth."

"My fault?" Tres's nostrils flared. "I didn't push you over that cliff."

"No, you were too busy trying to steal my soulmate. Again. You might as well have kicked me over the edge."

"You're never going to forgive me for that," Tres sighed.

"Maybe when you stop trying to do it," said Zane.

Tres opened his mouth to respond, but Loren cut him off.

"Wait," she said, holding up her hands for all conversation to cease. "I have to ask the most important question of the day."

We all faced her. Her face was grave as she looked out at the energy weave of a window.

"What," she began, "in god's name"—she turned to me—"are you wearing?"

All eyes swiveled from Loren to me. I smoothed my hands over the wrinkled, plain sheath that covered my body.

"It's all Eden had available," I said, my voice nearing a whine. "It was this or naked."

"Which reminds me..." Loren's short attention span hopped from me to Zane. "... I didn't get a hug, Frenchie."

I stepped between Zane's nude body and Loren.

"What?" She shrugged innocently. "I'll mind the boundaries." She peered around me for another look. "Though that would be a wide gap between us."

Zane laughed good-naturedly.

Tres's features clouded over, his jaw tense. "If we hadn't come down here, you two would still be assed out. Literally."

"And now your ass is trapped with ours," said Zane.

Tres's shoulders deflated. "I figured that might be a possibility."

"Yet you came for her anyway?" said Zane.

Tres turned and stared at Zane as though he was an idiot. "You really think I would leave you in harm's way?"

Zane cocked his head. The affirmative was clearly written on his face.

"Okay." Tres huffed. "I may have done that before. But I've always come back for you. Haven't I?"

Zane cocked his head in the other direction.

"Come on, Zayin. That was one time. I have never left you in a situation that would've led to your demise. When I've caused you to get maimed, I've always come back to make amends. Eventually."

Zane took a deep breath and his face relaxed.

Tres put out his hand, palm open.

Zane looked at the open palm for long seconds before extending his own. The moment Zane's palm touched Tres's, Tres pulled him in for a hug, gap be damned.

"We really are brothers?" said Tres.

"It would appear so," said Zane as they parted.

"I always suspected as much."

"Our father is a dick," said Zane.

"I noticed."

"So, I can't blame you for how you turned out." Zane turned away from Tres before he spoke again. "I would've come for you, too."

"I know," said Tres. He shoved his hands in his pockets. "I did have a doubt. But I had more hope than doubt."

"Aww, look, Nia. The bromance is back on," said Loren. "Now that everyone has made up, let's stop wasting time and get out of here. The rest of my family's up there on the surface. And I will not have some prejudiced angels hurt them because they're specists."

Loren turned to the solid door. She stared at it, perplexed. She reached out her hand, and just like that, the door to the cage opened.

Wow. Maybe my bestie was more powerful than I thought. But no. Of course it wasn't that simple.

CHAPTER THIRTEEN

*E*den glided into the room, her feet bare like the rest of her. Behind her, Michael stood at her right hand and Gabriel at her left. Both males looked impassive as they came into the room. Neither made eye contact with the room's inhabitants.

Eden looked around the room, her head slanting to the left and then to the right as she regarded each one of us in turn. Finally, she found Loren.

Loren stood beside me. Tres had an arm outstretched, as though ready to block Eden's assault or Loren's charge. I'm not quite sure which he anticipated.

"I'm told that what you did could be interpreted

as brave," Eden began, her address aimed solely at Loren. "Breaking into a forbidden realm, stealing a deity's prized possession, incurring the wrath of his warrior daughters, and then trying to repeat the same tactics in my realm."

Loren raised her chin. Tres moved closer to her side. That gesture, I knew, was a protective one. I moved closer to her with Zane at my back. But still, standing in the presence of God and her angels felt like I was in nursery school being scolded by the headmistress after I did something naughty.

"That does not compute to bravery to me," Eden was saying. "It is the very definition of insanity."

Tres bobbed his head in agreement. Then went still as a cockroach spotted on a wall when Loren and I glared at him.

"You do crazy things for your family," Loren said.

Eden's golden eyes flashed at her. Her head pitched to the side in curiosity. "But you don't share any light or blood with these Ishim."

"Friends are the family you choose," said Loren. "It's the choice that makes the bond stronger with each passing day."

Eden considered that. Her eyes went unfocused and her lips pursed together.

"Besides," continued Loren, "I thought all god's

creatures were connected. At least that's what the New Age hipsters are preaching these days."

Eden chuckled. "I like her. Are there more of them like her on the surface?"

"God, no," coughed Tres.

"Why don't you go up and see for yourself," I suggested.

Eden wrinkled her nose. "Humans make such a fuss when I go up. And they always seem to misinterpret what I say. What is this nonsense I hear about a woman, a serpent, and an apple?"

We all looked around at each other. But no one offered up an explanation for the myth of Original Sin. Out of the four of us, I was likely the most religious. Not because I practiced any faith. I just knew the most about the systems of human beliefs, having recorded their inner workings. Truthfully, none of the spiritual practices had ever made any sense to me.

I suppose this was why. I'd been born into and grew up in the presence of deities. They weren't supernatural to me. They were natural, normal. Now that I remembered them. Maybe if humans were given the chance to interact with the Elohim more, they would calm their destructive behaviors a bit.

"Humans have always sought your guidance,

Eden," I said. "For as long as I've been recording their stories, they've related what they believe you want them to do. They've come close to getting it right, but they keep missing the mark. I think if you just spent more time with them, or if you wrote your instructions yourself and I took them above ground then—"

"No," said Eden. "It is already decided. The time of humans has come to an end. They've become too dangerous, their rebellion too great. I hate to lose any of my creatures, but if they continue to exist, it could mean the end to us all."

"You're a cold-hearted bitch."

The collective gasp was so forceful it sucked the air out of the room. Everyone turned and gaped at Loren.

"It's true," said Loren. "You wanna see insane, look no further than her daughters. And I see why they're that way now that I've met their mother. She neglects them as she does humanity and all life on the surface. Yet she expects them to know what to do without any instruction. And when they call out to you, you ignore them."

Eden's lips parted. That was the only tell she even paid attention to Loren. Other than her slightly parted lips, nothing else on her person moved.

"You're a horrible mother," said Loren. "To the Valkyrie and to the human race."

"She has a point," Tres said. "Humans have no knowledge of the real god. No wonder all of creation acts out. It's your fault, all of your fault, not theirs."

"Humans didn't grow inside of you." Zane joined the chorus. "So you wouldn't know love. You don't know what it is to have life inside, only on the outside."

"Close your mouths, both of you," snarled Michael. We all jerked at his words. His face transformed from its apathetic countenance into something dark and, dare I say, devilish. The words he aimed at his sons carried a vicious threat.

"You have no right to ask anything of us," said Zane. "You've been just as absent to us as she's been to all her children. That's what's wrong. The problem is you all. I had a mother. We all did. We grew in her womb. Once we were outside, our mothers taught us, guided us in love. We weren't born fully formed like Elohim. We were born connected to our mothers and that's how we learned love."

Zane looked to me. My heart quickened for this man. My pulse caught in my throat when his fingers found mine. When our fingers entwined, my temperature rose.

"Nova's right," he continued. "Humans don't know you. Not really. They tell stories. But Mother is the name of god for every child. Family, and that bond, is what is worshipped and fought over and died for. But you wouldn't understand that. You sent us up to the surface to do your bidding. You left us with no instruction. And then you condemn us when we don't do your bidding."

Eden's golden eyes sparkled, but her blank expression was unreadable. Her attention flicked to her side, to Michael. I'm not sure if it was a signal for permission or a sign of resignation.

Michael raised his hand, as though urging Zane to back down. Zane didn't take a step back. His body jerked up into the air. Pain shot through me as Zane's limbs stretched and he was yanked away from me.

From his suspended place hanging in the air, Zane's skin turned sallow. Wrinkles creased the soft skin under his hazel eyes and spread downward. Like a disease, the depressions rippled down his neck to his chest, out to his forearms until it extended to gnarl and bend his fingertips.

For thousands of years, Zane had appeared the

picture of health. Now he was an old, decrepit man who could barely lift his head. My heart dropped like lead and I couldn't move. Not to him, not away from him to hurl myself at his maker, the one who was the cause of all this pain.

Luckily, his brother was on it. With a warrior's cry, Tres charged Michael. His big body barreled forward until it reached the being of light.

Michael didn't even flinch. He barely raised his other hand. With the slight motion, Tres's body jerked upward in the same fashion as Zane's.

Instead of aging Tres, Michael attacked his heart. He went for his strength. Tres's bulging biceps deflated like balloons losing air. His broad chest went concave and he sank into himself.

"Flesh is weak," said Michael. "If you want to be strong, you'll stand in the light."

I tried to find my voice, but my throat was dry. I could barely get a breath in, much less push any out to make sound. I was absolutely paralyzed. Was one of them holding me?

I looked to my father. His gaze was on the floor. But slowly, as though he felt the heat of scrutiny, his eyes raised to me. Only briefly. And then I saw it. His left eye twitched, just slightly, but it moved.

I'd never been one to ask a man to do my dirty

work for me. But I knew in the bottom of my soul that this was a battle I couldn't win on my own. If I twitched a muscle, I'd end up like Zane and Tres. I wanted them restored, and it looked like only my father could do that for me.

Unfortunately, even though his eye twitched, Gabriel's gaze quickly fell away from mine. His eyes glazed over in that impassive mask, just as they had done when he'd watched my mother's flesh and bones go up in flames.

He would not help me. It was up to me. But, of course, there was Loren.

Loren pulled out her sword from her bag, and I loved her for it. I also hated her for it. She moved when my body refused. She raced into battle when I sought a negotiation. She threw caution to the wind where I tried to make calculations. And she proved my prudence right.

She didn't even have a chance to brandish the blade before she joined the men. With a flick of his head, Michael tossed her body up to join Zane and Tres. Instead of aging her or weakening her, he brought plague and pestilence upon her.

Loren's beautiful face dotted with pockmarks. Blood tinted her clear blue eyes. The red liquid pooled in the corners and she blinked tears of blood. That final sight pushed me to action.

I fell to my knees. My head bowed in supplication. My shoulders drooped in defeat.

"Please," I whispered.

"Please," I begged.

"Please," I cried.

Back on the surface, I had a cave of the most precious things in the world to me. I'd guarded it fiercely for years. I'd give it all up now. Now, when the three people I held most dear in my life were in dire straits.

I raised my head to Eden. She was my only hope. I knelt before her, weaponless, defenseless, completely at her mercy.

"Please."

Eden had been looking away, beyond the window, at the lush life outside the golden threads of the cage. When I spoke, her pointy ears perked up. Her bright eyes slowly found mine, still not looking at Michael's dirty work.

"Do you think I enjoy this?" she asked.

I didn't respond. I couldn't see past the pain in my chest that connected me to Zane. I couldn't think past the contortions of Tres's face. I couldn't get past Loren's roiling anger.

"Life is precious," said Eden. "No one knows that better than I. No one has ever been by themselves, truly alone. Only me."

"They are precious to me."

"You think me unfeeling? You think me uncaring? I will sacrifice the many to save the few. Otherwise, we may all perish."

"What do you want?" I said.

She didn't answer. She'd already asked the question. She was here for an answer.

"I'll do it," I said. "I'll work for you. I'll help you choose humans to live. But they are my first choice. You have to let them live. I'll only do it if you let them live. Otherwise, there's no purpose for me." My voice broke on the plea.

"We're not so different, you and I," she said.

There wasn't any animosity as she considered me. There was a heaviness, and it made me sick because I didn't want to sympathize with her. I was nothing like her.

"I am not the villain," she said. "I am the savior."

There was a loud thunk as the three bodies fell to the floor. Michael left without a backwards glance. Gabriel looked straight ahead, steadily avoiding my gaze before he followed Eden out. As they left through the opaque door, it never darkened. They left our cage wide open. It didn't matter, now that our spirits were broken.

CHAPTER FOURTEEN

I turned away from the open door and back to my friends. My hands found Zane and I wrapped my arms around him. Pushing his unruly locks out of my way, I got a clear view of his face.

His flesh was as smooth as the day he was reborn. Not a wrinkle or blemish marred his perfect face, neck, or torso. His eyes remained closed as he heaved in a deep breath that I felt in my chest.

"I'm sorry," I said to Zane.

"What sin have you committed lately?" He winced through a grin.

"I keep putting you in harm's way."

"Well, yeah. This relationship does often lend itself to a bit of bondage and sadism."

I wanted to punch him, but that would prove his point that I was always hurting him. I could still feel the agony from his father's cruelty leaving his body. Instead, I cradled his head at my bosom.

"You are forgiven," he said as he nuzzled into my breasts.

I held him tighter. We'd been in hairy situations before, but there had never been one I didn't believe we'd live through. I'd had my doubts when he'd been suspended in pain.

Michael had proven his point. Flesh was weak and easily manipulated. Zane was the light in my heart. He was a part of me. That bond no one could ever break.

"They go through me before they get to you," Zane said. "I will always be at your back. Even when you're pissed at me and push me away. Even when I'm livid with you and turn you away. It's always been that way between us. Between us all."

Zane looked over my shoulder. I followed the trajectory of his gaze. Tres's face came into view.

Zane and Tres didn't exchange words. Just one of those silent nods of understanding between men. The nod told Zane and me that Tres stood as solidly behind that statement as we both did. Even if the two men were fighting and arguing and at each other's throats, they'd always had and always would have each other's backs. Tres's eyes let me know I was included in that pact.

Tres's cheeks were full once more, as were the strength of his biceps and the expanse of his chest. His arms and chest were filled with a certain blonde witch. Tres cradled Loren like the precious thing she was.

I felt a pang of jealousy. Not of Loren for being in Tres's arms. I was jealous that Tres, not I, comforted my bestie.

Jealousy fled when a wretched sound came from Loren's throat. Her shoulders shook up and down as she sobbed.

I let go of Zane and reached for my best friend. Tres didn't immediately let her go. Begrudgingly, he relinquished his hold on her. But she didn't let him go.

"Loren?" I ran my hand tenderly through her mussed strands. Had Michael not set her to rights? Was the disease still wracking her body? Had that ass-light left scars?

Slowly, Loren lifted her head. There were spots on her face. Red spots from where her face had met the buttons on Tres's shirt. Her eyes were still red. Her cheeks were puffy.

She looked miserable. Michael would pay. I didn't know how yet, but I'd figure something out. No one messes with my best friend and gets away with it.

"I can't let them die, Nia," Loren said.

She gulped down a lungful of air. She shifted from Tres's hold and came into mine. Even when she was on her deathbed she hadn't cried.

"They're my family," she continued. "I have to protect them."

Loren meant the witches and knights of Camelot. They were her blood relations. I knew she had my back, just as Zane and Tres did. We were the family she had chosen. But the connection with the people of Camelot was instant and even deeper with her.

I was connected to them as well. Igraine had been the closest thing I'd had to a mother this past millennium. I'd grown closer to Morgan and Gwin now that they were older. Even Arthur had grown on me now that we weren't at each other's throats. And those were just a few of the connections I'd made in my time on Earth.

There were humans, past and present, whose acquaintance I didn't want to lose before their time was rightly up. There were even animals that held tender spaces in my heart. And don't get me started on the structures and artifacts and land on the surface. And all those museums. What about the things not yet unearthed?

No.

This apocalypse could not happen. It would not happen. Not while I still drew breath.

There was a way out. There had to be. There always was.

Loren sniffled. Her eyes were so forlorn, it broke my heart all over again. I grasped both of her shoulders and gave her a shake.

"You silly twit," I said. "You really thought I was giving up."

"Well, yeah," she said. "Not that I blame you. Watching the three people I love most in the world being torn apart, that would have felled me, too."

"I already fell and died once. They just showed me the worst they can do. And we're all still standing."

But we weren't standing. We were all slumped on the floor.

"Okay, we're all sitting. They may have wiped the dinosaurs off the face of the Earth, run the fae to another realm, but they just messed with the wrong life forms. No one messes with my bestie."

I gave Loren's arm a squeeze. "Or my man." I turned to Zane. Then I faced Tres. "Or my... brother?"

"No." Tres grimaced. "No." He spat the word emphatically.

"Okay, not brother," I conceded, raising my hands in defeat. "We can figure that out later. But they just messed with the wrong family."

"Hell, yeah," said Loren.

"I have been a voice for the silenced and forgotten for as long as I've been on the surface. I'm not gonna turn my back now. I can't. I couldn't live with myself."

Tres shook his head. He might not have been immediately on board with my rallying speech. But when he lifted his head, his brown eyes might as well have been steel. There was the Broody Billionaire that made CEOs cry.

Tres looked beyond me, and his gaze locked with Loren's. She took a deep breath and held his gaze. Her shoulders steeled. Her back arched and her boobs lifted, a clear sign she was battle-ready.

Zane wrapped his arm around me, pulling me back into his embrace. I took his comfort, his strength, his support. We were down but we were not out.

"We're not giving up," I said. "We're getting out of here."

"But... how?" said Loren.

"It's us against God," said Tres. "And a legion of angels."

"It's going to take a miracle to get us out of here," said Zane.

And just like that, a figure appeared in the open door. Of course, she appeared in the doorway looking for me. She was my family, the only person in the world who shared my blood.

Vau's eyes were wide with surprise at the open door. She had some gadget in her hand. I had to assume, from her shock at the easy access, that the gadget's purpose had been to free us. Vau's chest rose and sank in relief when she saw me on the floor.

The corners of my eyes crinkled as tears pooled, knowing she'd come for me. Her forehead creased into lines that could only mean *As if I'd be anywhere else when you were in danger.*

She quickly made her way toward me but paused a few feet away. "Gil? Is that you?"

In the time Vau had known Tres, he was called Gilgamesh, the great ruler of Sumer.

"Vau?" said Tres. "Is that you?"

Tres rose and embraced Vau. Then he was

engulfed in a bear hug by Epsilon, the only male slightly larger than him.

"We came to rescue you," said Vau. "But the door's open."

"Eden unlocked our cage," I said.

"Then why are you still here?" Vau asked.

"Well, we don't have a plan yet. Why are you rescuing us? I thought you agreed with the Elohim."

"We do," said Vau. "But not like this. I've never cared for revenge. Humans are awful. No offense," she said to Loren.

"I'm half witch," said Loren, "so I'm only a little offended."

"We chose to live apart from them," Vau continued. "But I believe there's room for all of Eden's creatures. I believe there's a possibility for redemption, maybe even improvement, especially with the young."

"If only you weren't the only ones who believed that," I said.

"We're not," said Vau. "There are others. Come with us."

CHAPTER FIFTEEN

No one stopped us as we left our gilded cage. No one glanced at us. In fact, Elohim and other beings—the extinct and the rare entities—parted as we walked out.

Why would they have tried to stop us? They'd have no reason to. No one defied Eden or her angels.

Eden was all-powerful, but not innocent. She said she did what was necessary for all, but she had avoided witnessing Michael's assault on his own children. She had displayed something like sadness when she spoke of the plight of the dragons and the dinosaurs. She had turned away when harm had been done to my friends in that cage of a room.

Speak of the devil, I spied Eden a distance away. She stood before the dragon her daughter had ridden. I supposed Bryn hadn't listened to her mother and still hung around somewhere below the surface. Likely just to spite her mother for her inattentiveness.

Atta girl. Not that I was warming to the Valkyrie. But I certainly understood her misbehavior a bit better now.

The dragons had defied the Elohim. For their stance, their rebellion had been nipped in the bud and the roots of their kind had been torn out. The majestic beasts were reduced to domesticated conveyances now.

My steps slowed as I continued to watch Eden. She approached the dragon. Her footfalls appeared heavy even from this distance.

She reached out, a warm glow emitting from her palm. The massive dragon could've blasted her to bits. It could've chomped down and swallowed her with one gulp. It could've batted her into the stalactites with one sweep of its spikey tail.

Instead, it bowed its head. Its long, sinewy neck bent down to receive her touch. Its large eyelids shut, a sign of both trust and gratitude.

Eden bent her forehead to the great beast. More warmth glowed from where their crowns met. Was the embrace the dragon's sacrament or Eden's benediction? I couldn't tell, but neither could I look away.

My ragtag group of rebels were a few steps ahead of me. They marched into battle, preparing to stand behind a cause I championed. Zane paused his advance and looked around until he spotted me behind him, but he didn't come to me. One by one, each of my friends stopped and looked back for me.

What was I doing? We couldn't win this battle. I couldn't save humanity. I wasn't sure I could save those who lined up with me. This rebellion had shown its inevitable trajectory when Michael had barely lifted a finger to stop us. My father and Eden did nothing to stop him.

But my friends' eyes showed determination. They were not backing down. Whatever happened, we'd do it together.

I loved each person who stood in front of me. I'd go down fighting for the connections we all shared. Otherwise, what was the purpose of life?

Zane held out his hand to me. I entwined his fingers with mine. Tres and I exchanged a glance and a nod. Loren brushed up beside me, wrapping her arm with mine.

"They're over there," said Vau.

She pointed to a small crowd of Elohim off to the

side under one of the open structures. They slowly moved away from the structure, leaving two beings behind. It took me a moment to recognize who Vau pointed to. But when I saw the two identical faces, I knew what I had to do.

I let go of Zane and marched up to Hunahpú and Xbalanqué. The God Twins were larger than life below ground as above. To me, it had only been a day since I'd last seen them. But apparently weeks had passed since that encounter.

One of them saw me coming, but the one who faced away spoke. I supposed what one saw, so did the other. "We told you not to go through the door, little Ishim."

"You should've listened to us," said the other twin, the one looking me over.

"That's not what you said," I protested. "Not exactly."

The twin who had kept his back to me turned. He looked me over with a salacious smile. But I didn't worry about my virtue. I knew I wasn't his type. Too much light in my veins, where they liked their women with a little more flesh and blood.

"You didn't listen," he said.

"What does it matter?" said his brother.

I had trouble telling them apart. In all honesty I

couldn't tell which was which when I'd walked up to them. It didn't matter.

"What matters now is that Eden is going to exterminate humanity," I said.

"It's what the purists do," said one of the God Twins. "Eden experiments and Michael cleans up after her."

"Cleans up?" said the other brother. "More like gets rid of the competition."

"Competition?" Loren asked.

Like the leeches they were, both twins zeroed in on her. A smile spread across their deceptively youthful faces. In that moment, they looked exactly like their shifter sons, the Mohegan twins. I'd seen panties drop when Chak and Saka split their lips into wide grins.

But not with my Loren. Loren raised an eyebrow at them, cool enough to chill the light beings. Which was odd. She was never above using her feminine wiles to get her way. But I supposed this was a stressful time, and she was solely focused on her family.

One of the God Twins, perhaps because he saw he'd have to work for it, gave up the pursuit and spilled the beans. "Before the dragons, there were the beasts of the sea. But you only spy a few of those from time to time in lochs or out in the deep ocean. Millions of years ago, life in the primordial seas easily outnumbered those that walked on the earth. There's only a fraction of the original sea life left. And most are docile."

"What are you saying?" I asked. Because I had no idea.

"Michael doesn't like competition," said the other twin. "He believes in exclusivity. When the dragons emerged as the dominant species of the dinosaurs, Michael saw a threat to his livelihood, his authority. Ever hear of the saying *thin the herd?* It was around before humans began hunting deer."

"But I thought the dragons rebelled?" I said.

"Yes. They did. I'm sure you would too if you were told your kind needed to undergo population control."

Eden had said that I could choose a few humans to save. Wasn't that a form of population control? Weren't we now rebelling?

"She's getting the picture," said one brother to the other.

"Fire and brimstone rained down and the world was cast into darkness," said the other brother. "The fae left before the smoke and ice cleared. They were fearful they would be next on Michael's hit list."

"But Eden has to see what he's doing," I said.

"Not likely," said Tres. "She doesn't even pay attention to her own daughters."

"And," said Zane, "she admitted she rarely goes to the surface to check on her creations."

What a mess. The world was about to be exterminated because its mother was too busy working late.

"You have to help us," I said to the twins.

"We don't have to do anything," they said in unison.

"Eden's going to let Michael wipe out all of humanity. That means all of your progeny. Your children, the Balam and Mohegan."

"It wouldn't be the first time," said one twin. But he looked away when he said it, not meeting my gaze. Meanwhile, his brother looked skyward.

"So, you're okay with it happening again?" I asked.

They said nothing.

"This was a waste of time," Loren huffed.

"You can't stop them," said one twin. "Anyone who rebels is wiped out of existence. Eden's probably anticipating your move now. The word omnipotent doesn't mean she sees all. It means she has ultimate power. She can do whatever she wants."

I shook my head in the negative. She did not have all the power. Not while we still had breath. "There has to be something? At least help us get out of here. Let us through one of your doorways to the surface. Then we can warn our loved ones. Get them to safety. Or high ground. Or low ground. Something."

The brothers didn't immediately say no and hope sprang in my heart. But then one of them sighed. The other one's broad shoulders drooped. "There are no doors to the surface opening for many cycles."

I wasn't willing to admit defeat. None of us were. There had to be a way.

"You could get out through the seas," said one twin. "But the temperature is a few hundred degrees. It will burn your flesh away and kill your halfling friend."

"But," said Vau, "the Elohim don't need a door to leave."

"You're right," I said. "You two put that star door system into place after the Ishim were born. How did Elohim get to the surface before that?"

"Oh," said one of the brothers. "There is that way."

We all waited for him, or the other one, to finish the statement.

"How?" I shouted into their prolonged silence.

"You won't like it," said one brother. He looked at me and Zane. "It's going out the way you two came in."

He was right. I didn't like that idea. That way had hurt like death. Because it had been death. But if I could save the ones I loved, I'd just have to do it again.

"How do we get there?" I asked.

"The way is through Eden's lab."

CHAPTER SIXTEEN

We left the open-air structure and the God Twins behind. They didn't exactly wish us well. I'm not sure they believed our attempts would work. I wouldn't be surprised if they would soon be taking bets with some of the Elohim on whether or not we'd succeed. Five Ishim and a witch against a dozen ancient beings of light? I didn't like our odds.

The six of us came to the structure that housed Eden's lab. A crowd of Elohim stood outside. Once again, Michael stood at the center of them. Gabriel stood just beyond him, staring into the distance as though he wasn't really listening to Michael's speech.

I didn't blame him. Michael spoke in a

monotone, passionless voice. It would've put me to sleep if his words weren't so vile.

"Humans are crowding every bit of the globe," said Michael. "Wherever they touch the surface, it runs fallow. Their numbers have multiplied beyond what can possibly be sustainable by the Earth's resources. They take and give nothing in return, which makes them parasites. This is our world. They only exist by our leave. If we allow the scourge to continue, there will be nothing left of our world."

Michael paused and looked around at the assembled crowd. I waited for a dissenter. Not a single one spoke up.

"We thought these beings were evolving," Michael continued. "But in truth, the species has been abating. Humans barely have any light to their persons. They are primarily water and flesh. And yet these are the beings that are meant to inherit the Earth?"

Again, silent acquiescence as Michael paused and eyed the onlookers. Gabriel still looked off to the side with apparent disinterest. The only ones who bristled were the non-Elohim. Tres had an arm around Loren's waist. Zane's arms were wrapped around my shoulders.

"It is time the Earth's first children reclaim our birth right and retake the surface."

That drew a series of nods from one corner of the crowd. But still most of the Elohim watched impassively. Tres's hold tightened on Loren. Vau looked from Epsilon to me, her features grave.

I turned to Zane. I wasn't sure if I was seeking comfort or preparing to bark out orders. I couldn't do either. He pressed his soft lips against mine.

The kiss wasn't passion-filled. There was no message in it like goodbye. It could've been an ordinary, any day kiss, if this wasn't the last day for humanity on Earth.

"Guys," said Loren. "Now is not the time."

Zane pulled away from me. His brown eyes were soft on me. His lips, so soft a moment ago, firmed into a determined line.

"I know that look," Tres said.

"So do I," I said.

"What's going on?" asked Loren.

"I'm about to go and get punched in the face for love," Zane said.

"Wait," Vau said.

Zane paused and faced her. She came into his arms and embraced him. "This feels like goodbye," he said.

"It is," Vau said. "Properly this time."

"You're not coming with us?" I asked.

Vau released Zane and then took me into her arms. "This is where we belong. When things die down, or you die again, you can come visit."

Letting her go was harder than I'd thought it would be. But she was right. At least we got to say goodbye this time. We all exchanged hugs, Epsilon and me, and then Epsilon and Tres and Zane. Vau also gave Tres a peck on the cheek.

"Take care of her," Vau said to Loren. "Stop her from doing anything too stupid. You know the boys won't."

Loren nodded. She got a hug from Vau too. Then Vau and Epsilon walked off into the light. We stood and watched, though they never disappeared behind a valley or a dip in the flat land.

Finally, Zane took a deep breath and took off toward his father before I could stop him. A couple of steps later, Tres was on his brother's heel.

"Michael," Zane called. "May I have a word?"

Michael glanced at his son. "I'm in the middle of planning an apocalypse. Can it wait until after humanity has been wiped from the face of the Earth?"

"That's what I want to talk with you about," said Zane.

"Are you going to ask for leniency?"

"For mankind? No. But I did want to try and save a few priceless pieces of art."

"Art?" Michael's nose crinkled as he tested the word and found it sour. "Sculpted rock and splattered bits of dye?"

Zane bristled. "Art is the expression of inner light."

"I don't have time to save etchings and structures," said Michael.

"Wait?" said Tres. "Structures? I've spent my life building structures. Those should not be on the chopping block. What has a temple or a shrine or a skyscraper ever done to disrupt the earth?"

"They'll be dust in centuries," said Michael.

"Not my buildings," said Tres.

The arrogant engineer was on full display next to the optimistic artist. But then Zane turned to Tres, ire in his eyes.

"Excuse me," said Zane. "I was talking to our father. Your buildings aren't more important than my art."

"I beg to differ," said Tres. He pushed his

shoulders back, as though readying himself for a fight. Zane did not disappoint.

"You always do this." Zane poked Tres in the shoulder.

Tres stumbled back a couple of steps. He reached up and brushed off the spot on his shoulder where Zane had touched him. Then he dug his heels in, preparing to charge.

Michael looked at his two sons in confusion. The gathered Elohim watched the exchange, their large eyes just a touch wider than normal. I turned away from the melee. I knew exactly what the two men were on about.

"Loren," I said. "Come on. This is the diversion."

It was hard to look away from the man I loved. But it had to be done. I needed to find a way into Eden's lab and then that doorway of death. Zane and I might be separated again, but I knew it wouldn't be the last time.

"I've never understood this emotion." Michael's voice carried to where Loren and I were dashing away. "Love? It goes against self-preservation to put someone else before you. It's not natural."

The hairs at the back of my neck prickled. I knew I should go forward, but I couldn't help it. I turned back. Michael wasn't focused on his sons and their grievances. He was looking directly at me.

And so was my father. Gabriel's eyes darted between Michael and me. And then I caught it, the slightest twitch of his left eye. Gabriel didn't move toward me. Michael did.

Michael's skin began to dissipate. I knew what that meant. Where it took a moment for flesh to make its way across distances, light traveled instantaneously.

"Loren, run."

We took off, moving as fast as our bodies would allow us. The light door to Eden's lab was opaque, announcing that it was open. And why wouldn't it be? No one here would defy her.

Loren and I dashed inside the lab. I felt Michael's heat at my back. We crossed the threshold, but there was no door to shut.

Rays of light wrapped around my shoulder. I struggled, throwing punches and kicking my feet. But to no avail. The rays of light held me still, rooting me in place.

"Calm yourself, child."

The voice was monotone and passionless. But it wasn't Michael's voice. The rays loosened enough for me to turn and face my father's bright eyes.

"Let me go," I said.

Gabriel shook his head. "You'll only hurt yourself. This is for the best."

Seriously? Thousands of years with no parental guidance and now he was trying to keep me from doing the most important thing in the world.

"You are more important than they are."

"Get out of my head," I shouted. "You're cold and heartless and I hate you."

That left eye definitely twitched this time. The cool wind of a huffed breath from Gabriel's flaring nostrils brushed against me. But still, he did not let me go.

Eden appeared through the doorway. "I can't say I didn't expect this. It's happened before, you know. But I had hoped you'd weave a different pattern."

"Did you ever think that you're what's wrong with the pattern?" I asked.

"There's always someone like you," Eden said instead of answering me. "Something like you—a pocket of energy that burns bright with the fires of righteousness. It vexes me when you stand before me. But I miss you when you're gone. Complacency does not improve an entity. True evolution only happens when there is adversity."

"Like rebellion?" I said.

"Adversity is pushing. Rebellion involves mutiny. But I forgive you."

She reached out to me, much like she'd done with the dragon. But I didn't lean into her and seek her warmth or forgiveness.

Eden sighed, but she didn't move away from me. "I hate this part."

"Hate is a strong emotion," I said. "You don't like emotions."

"Hatred is warm." Eden nodded. "It burns and leaves scars. You don't hate me. You'd like to. But you like me, just as I like you."

"I don't like what you're doing," I said. "I can't reconcile that you do it with no feeling."

"I do it with knowledge. Knowing it is for the best. Not the best for me, but the best for us all. You can't see it. No one can see it. But I can."

"I can only see that you're hurting people, your creation."

Eden opened her mouth to protest, but then closed it. That caught me off guard. Had I stumped god?

"Um, guys?"

All eyes turned to Loren. She'd made it to the center of the lab without detection. They'd misjudged her, likely assumed she was beneath their notice. Big mistake.

"What's this orb thingy?" Loren asked. "It looks important."

Eden's eyes widened. Michael, who had come in behind Eden, tensed his jaw. Gabriel, who still held me tight in his arms, exhaled on a choked breath.

"Put that down," said Eden.

"Let my friends go," said Loren.

Michael lifted his hand, likely preparing to wreak havoc on Loren's body again.

"Ah ah," tsked Loren. "Pull one of those aging or muscle weak things and I'm liable to drop this."

Eden put her hand up in front of Michael. Michael put his down.

"I believe we have what's called a Mexican stand-off." Loren tossed the globe up like a ball, one-handed. I know she aimed to catch it. But the orb wasn't like a ball. "Oops."

All eyes watched as the nucleus went up a few inches in the air. Then all eyes watched as it came back down in her palm... and rolled off the ridge of her hand.

And then, for the second time, there was a loud crash all around us.

CHAPTER SEVENTEEN

The ground shifted again. I fell to my knees as the ground beneath my bare feet quaked. The walls of the lab shook and a few of the glass containers hurtled toward the floor.

But not a single enclosure crashed to the earth. Fast as lightning, Eden darted and dove. She caught one, and then another, and then placed them on a solid surface. Then she sprang up and dipped low to catch more as the seismic shifts continued.

She moved so fast, the room seemed to bend around her. Particles flew past her, moving out of her way so that she could save her precious specimens. While Eden was busy on her rescue mission, I realized we had an opening.

Loren had fallen to the floor when the orb had

slipped through her fingers. Michael was scrambling over to the sphere, trying to scoop it into his arms. But with every bounce of the sphere, the core of the earth shook. Each time the earth shook, the sphere bounced away.

Luckily for me, Loren wasn't so bouncy. I grabbed her, and the two of us scrambled to the opaque doorway. Gabriel was near enough to grab for me, to bring me back into captivity. He remained in a crouch, his gaze affixed on me.

I turned away from my father. Whether I imagined his apathy or not, he would not receive any gratitude from me for letting us escape. Thanks was reserved for those who took action to assist. He'd done nothing but obstruct my hopes and dreams since we'd been reunited.

As the earth shook again, a rock fell in front of the door of light. The boulder was taller than me. Loren and I would have to climb over it. And still a shower of rocks of various sizes rained down.

Arms came around me. I looked up, expecting to see Zane's face. It wasn't his dark head or honey-golden arms. Instead, my father lifted me in his arms.

"No," I shouted, reaching for Loren.

Gabriel frowned, as though I were a whining

toddler reaching for her favorite toy. But in the end, he hefted Loren up with his other hand and lifted us both up and over the blockage. I allowed a bit of appreciation to seep into my heart.

"What's happening?" I said. "Has it begun? Is this Armageddon?"

"Your friend caused a tectonic shift," Gabriel said.

"How was I supposed to know that unguarded little ball would cause such a big problem?" said Loren.

We were on the other side of the lighted doorway and thrust into pandemonium. It was mayhem as trees swayed, their stiff limbs bending against their will. Some even fell to the ground. Beings of all shapes, sizes, and species ran for cover. Most of the Elohim had shed their skin and hovered above the ground. Still, that didn't save them from falling objects like tree limbs and rocks.

"Go," said Gabriel. "Now."

"But," I began. I didn't know what other words to add?

Thanks, Dad?
Come with us?
Did you do that because you love me?

"Now." Gabriel's voice brooked no argument. He

looked down at me with those expressionless eyes, and I swore I saw... something. Before I could name it, he turned and faded back into the lab.

Loren and I stayed low. Or at least we tried to. The moment we got outside, we were both lifted into the air.

Zane held me in his arms. He raced away from the destruction on sure feet. Just behind him was Tres, cradling Loren in his arms.

"Let me guess," said Tres. "This is Loren's doing."

"You don't know that," she said.

Tres grumbled in dissent, a sound I knew all too well.

The guys continued to race with us as we approached a cliff.

"There's no way out," said Loren. "Maybe we should just Thelma and Louise this?"

"No," shouted Tres. "I know that film and it ends with two women going over a cliff. There were no men. It's not going down like that."

"Put us down," I said. "We'll move faster if we're each only carrying our own weight."

The guys stopped. The moment they set us down, the Earth stilled. There was an eerie silence in the calm.

Then, without warning, the ground shook again.

But this time it was a localized event. A hand struck up from the rock, followed by another hand and then a head.

"You've got to be kidding me," said Loren. "Didn't we already vanquish this one?"

"I think we vanquished him to here," I said.

Cronus, the Titan father of the Greeks, extracted himself from the bowels of the earth. His dark shadow moved across the landscape and hovered over us. His dark, soulless eyes were fixed on us. Then he opened his large, gaping mouth.

"Climb inside," shouted Rhea.

Rhea had always been kind to me. She'd called upon me for help, so imagine my shock when she asked me and my loved ones to do the unthinkable.

"It's the only way," Rhea said. "Michael won't be able to detect you in there."

"You want us to climb inside the mouth of a filicidal god?"

"It's either that or climb the four thousand miles to the surface," said Cronus. "Your human friend here won't make it. The heat will rip the flesh from her mortal body. It'd be a waste of such a glowing soul."

Cronus's gaze was fixed on Loren's flushed skin. To remain on the surface, these gods had to consume human souls. Cronus had taken the practice too far, and his children had banished him to another realm. I guess this was that realm.

"He won't harm you," said Rhea. "I give you my word. You're the only hope for my children."

Tres jerked his head back like he was having an epileptic fit. "How is this any better than going over a cliff?"

"I don't think we have much choice," said Zane. "It's either our father or Zeus's."

"No, there's another way."

Once again, we all turned to face another familiar voice. It wasn't quite so unexpected to see her standing there, hand cocked on one hip, the other twirling her father's hammer. Bryn was just as pissed off at her parents as we were at ours.

"You'll help us?" I asked.

"Don't trust her," said Loren. "She's up to something."

Bryn cast Loren a sly look. "Of course I'm up to something. I should've joined you when you came to Asgard. You really know how to shake things up and get attention."

"Well." Loren sniffed and shrugged her shoulders without a modicum of modesty. "It's a gift."

I wasn't so easily swayed. There was that saying, better the devil you know than the one you don't. I knew what kind of devilry Cronus might bring, and I trusted Rhea to keep her husband in check. Mostly. She hadn't exactly been the one to free her children either time their daddy woke up hungry with a taste for magical flesh. I didn't know anything about Bryn. Except she had a bone to pick with her mother.

"Do you believe your mother is making a mistake with humanity?" I asked.

Bryn shrugged. "She's made mistakes before. Have you seen a platypus?"

Loren sniggered at the mention of the mismatched animal. Tres grimaced and shook his head in despair, likely mourning over the ill-conceived, ill-fitting proportions of the egg-laying mammal. Zane crossed his arms over his chest, looking affronted. He could find beauty in anything.

"Are you coming or not?" Bryn swung her father's hammer around in an arc. "I mean, unless you're gonna hitch a ride with the old Crone. Is that your stomach I hear growling, Croney?"

Cronus coughed and rubbed at his bare belly. In unison, we all took a step toward Bryn.

"Bryn," Eden's voice rang out.

Eden was moving in, flanked by dozens of

Elohim with Michael storming toward us in the lead. Gabriel was off to the side. Whatever emotion I thought I'd seen on his face was wiped clean, and he was back to his blank stare.

"Oh, hello, Mother," said Bryn. "Nice of you to come find me."

"I thought I told you to take that hammer back to your father," said Eden.

"You did. And I will. Just as soon as I finish my play date with my new friends."

Eden reached out her hand. Bryn held firm. The hammer didn't come flying into it like it had with Loren. Maybe something to do with Bryn being directly from Eden's essence.

"Let's talk about this, Bryn."

"Oh, now you have time to talk to me? Sorry, I'm going to hang out with my new friends. Don't wait up."

We all grabbed onto her as she swung her father's hammer. Bryn banged the hammer into the ground and set off another loud, crashing bomb. How much more would the Earth be willing to take from any of us?

CHAPTER EIGHTEEN

As the world exploded around me, the marrow in my bones vibrated. My skin was still very thin. The ringing of the hammer's impact caused the rays of my soul to undulate.

We flew up through darkness, but it wasn't entirely black. Particles danced in front of my nose. They looked much like those that had danced around Eden as she'd raced to save her specimens from true extinction. Still, with my skin so thin, it felt like parts of me were being torn away and I was falling to pieces.

But I didn't fall apart. Something solid held onto me. Something as familiar as my heartbeat.

Zane.

Like when he'd kissed me and held my hand,

and our essences touched. I felt him move through me. I felt us blend. It was a feeling of completion, of wholeness.

I'd never been one of those girls who thought a man, or even another living soul, had the ability to complete them. I had been a straight line all my life, traveling my own trajectory. Now, with him all around me, a part of me, I felt I'd come full circle traveling along a coordinated path.

Soon enough, the molecules coalesced. Blackness became bright. The ringing from the hammer's pound stopped. Zane and I broke apart, but he was still a part of me. Would always be.

I stepped out of his embrace and looked at my surroundings. The light wasn't exactly white. It was more purple with glows of pink. Just beyond where we stood was a castle with turrets rising to the sky. Before the castle was the statue of a man. He stood with one arm up in welcome. The other arm was extended down to hold the hand of a standing… mouse?

"Where are we?" I asked.

"The most magical place on Earth," answered Bryn. Her eyes glowed bright with enough amusement to rival the lights of the park. "I read all about it. There are fairies here, and knights, and enchanted castles. Surely we can mount an offensive here."

"This"—Loren spread her arms, but not in the welcoming fashion of the statue man—"is Disney World. You brought us to Disney World."

"Well," said Bryn, her brow crinkling with confusion. "Yes. There are many princesses and queens here. That's what we need. Royal women, warriors who will fight villains and protect their subjects."

"This is a place of make-believe," said Loren.

Bryn cocked her head in full confusion now. The move reminded me of her mother. Obviously being the daughter of God and from a family of warrior females, she'd run here instead of to the mostly male military present on each continent. She probably wouldn't believe us if we told her that men largely ruled the human world.

"Disney World is where families bring their children." Loren continued to try to explain Bryn's folly.

"Wait a minute," I said. "Where are all the families?"

The streets of Disney World were barren. Not a soul was at a concession stand or standing in a long line for a ride. But there wasn't total silence. A cacophony came from a distance.

"Where are the children?" Zane asked.

All the rides had stopped. No one stood in any of the shops. No one milled about. So where was the sound of raised voices coming from?

Dark clouds canvased the sky. I couldn't see a light, manmade or natural, beyond the strobes of Disney. It was as if the stars went out and the moon had disappeared.

Heaven will disappear with a roar.

Off in the distance, I heard a professional voice, stressed in its fake calm. A news reporter. I walked over to an array of flat screens in one of the outdoor eating areas.

"Take shelter now," said the anchorman. "The storm is coming. Meteorologists are having trouble categorizing it. It has exceeded the limits for a Category Five hurricane. This unprecedented monster storm has suddenly developed off the coast. It will hit Florida within the hour, reaching farther inland than we ever thought possible."

Screams soaked the air. They came from another television set, but they matched the muted cries we were hearing from somewhere inside the park. Or maybe not inside.

The second screen showed a bird's eye view of the scene just outside the gates of Disney. People were running in the streets. Cars careened to get out of the parking lot. There was a bottleneck at the gates, and panic ensued.

On another screen, satellite cameras captured a wall of water headed toward the Florida coast. The wall of water moved faster than I'd ever seen. It was unnatural.

It was the apocalypse.

"Oh, god," moaned Loren. "This is my fault. I dropped that orb thingy."

"It is not," I said. "They had the orb in hand when we left. They could've stopped it."

But that wall of liquid destruction wasn't stopping. It wasn't slowing down. The tip of it would hit the coast within the hour and slam far inward, very possibly touching Orlando. None of these people would even be able to get on the highway, much less get home. And this was just the beginning.

"What do we do?" asked Loren.

I opened my mouth, but no solutions came forth. I turned to Zane. As though we were twins, he opened his mouth in the same fashion. He didn't have any luck getting words out either. Instead, he pulled me close. I knew without him saying anything that he thought it was a hopeless cause, but he wouldn't leave my side.

Tres stood at Zane's shoulder while Loren stood at mine. A solid front against an indomitable army. Fight our way through a mass of assailants, sure. Take down destructive gods, not a problem. But put us in front of a wall of water, and we were helpless.

"So," Bryn said, "where's your army?"

No one answered. We all just stared bleakly at the screens depicting horror and chaos and impending doom.

"You do have an army, don't you?" Bryn said. "If not, this is going to be one lame, and quick, war."

An explosion blasted from somewhere near the Big Thunder Mountain Railroad. A ball of fire went up in the air. The spherical ball of fire sailed over to us.

Loren grabbed her sword. So did Bryn, bloodlust at the corner of her mouth. Tres broke apart a chair, coming away with two sharp stakes that were once chair legs. Zane opted for some steel railing spokes. I grabbed a steak knife from one of the dining tables—it was something. We might be going down, but it wouldn't be without a fight.

The fire ball landed a few feet in front of us. We

each dug our heels into the pavement and waited for the Elohim's assault.

Out of the fire stepped a small army that matched ours. First came a man in a debonair tailored suit. He was followed by a stylish woman in a couture dress that had me drooling. I didn't get to see the others, because Demeter, Greek Goddess of the Harvest, ran to me on her designer heels and embraced me.

"Nia, darling," cried Demi in her dramatic fashion. "Are we in time?"

"In time," I said as I caught a mouthful of her silky fabric. "In time for what? What are you all doing here?"

The rest of the Olympians had descended from Hades's fireball and stood before us. In addition to Demi and Desi were the perpetually serious Tia in a prim pantsuit, the golden-god himself, Zuzu, and his sister-bride Hera—just Hera, no nickname.

Bringing up the rear, dark tendrils radiated from Psi's head. But the God of the Sea wasn't alone. His hand was entwined with Viviane's, the Lady of the Lake. Wow, what had I missed while I'd been away?

"Our mother came to us in a dream," Demi said. "She said to come here on this date to help you. Something about another apocalypse or other."

"At least it's on this side of the globe," said Tia. "I do so hate all the clean-up that comes after floods and plagues."

I glared at the Greek Goddess of the Hearth. Immortals could be so callous. But Tia didn't notice my displeasure.

"I'm surprised it's happening so soon since the last time. When was that? Pompeii?" Tia took in the darkening weather and then focused on a handheld. "I suspected it wouldn't happen for another fifty to seventy-five years. I don't like when my calculations are off. I wonder what changed."

"Where've you been," said Demi. "We were supposed to go shopping two months ago. And it looks like I'm far too late."

Demi looked in despair at my simple, formless sheath, now covered in dust and debris from my escape from the center of the world. She reached out to the fabric, then pulled away at the last minute as though the material might bite her.

"She was grounded," said Loren. "You'd know that if you were her best friend. You'd also have come to rescue her from captivity if you were as close as you pretend to be."

"Listen," I said, coming between the two before

they could engage in this old battle. "We don't have time to argue now. A hurricane is coming."

"Oh?" said Demi. "Is that all? We can do something about that. Psi, darling?"

Psi came forward with Viviane. He gave me a wink as he nuzzled his cheek against Viviane's pale tresses.

"Hi-eee, Dr. Rivers," trilled Viviane. "What is up, Lady Lo?"

I looked from Viviane to Psi, who shrugged, to Loren, who raised her eyebrows in an admission of guilt.

"We were teaching her slang before she left for Rome on a shopping trip," said Loren. "Vivi, it looks like you got the shoes you wanted and a boyfriend."

"Soulmate," corrected Psi.

"Oh," I said with a nod of approval. "Congratulations, Viviane."

"I go by Vivi now." The Lady of the Lake waved her free hand at me. The other hand was entwined with Psi's. And the designer shoes on her feet were to die for. Man, I'd been gone that long?

A roil of thunder crackled overhead as the storm moved closer. The screams of people were still ever-present. The television screen showed little to no progress in getting the masses to safety. We needed to buy some more time.

"Zuzu," said Psi, "do something about that lightning storm, would you? Vivi and I will take care of that little storm out in the ocean."

Psi wrapped his arms around Vivi. He bent his knees and took off Superman-style. The two sea gods rose into the air on a stream of water, then went out of sight.

Zeus prepared to take off. Then he looked from me and Loren to Hera. Wariness clouded his handsome features. He wrapped his arms around Hera and carried her off into the darkness.

Smart man. We still had a bone to pick with that daddy's girl. Even more so now that her father had tried to make a meal of us again.

"There," said Demi. "All solved. So, we can go on that shopping trip now."

"We're still in the middle of the apocalypse, Demi. God, her name's Eden—wait, did you know that?"

Demi nodded. "Mother told us. We've never been to the core. So we've never met her. She seemed lovely by Mother's account."

"I swear, if the beings on this planet would simply communicate with each other, we'd save so much strife." I huffed. "Eden and the Elohim have decided that humans are more trouble than they're worth and they're going to wipe them off the face of the Earth."

That brought Tia's attention up from her handheld. "Humans are a life source to us. We can't survive without them. Not unless we are let down into the core to take sustenance directly from the light there."

"But I don't want to go to the core," said Demi. "They don't wear clothes down there."

True, that. I felt her pain. "We have to figure out a way to protect humanity."

"Against an army of the gods?" said Desi.

"If we want to keep our homes and livelihoods on the surface, then yes," I said.

"But how?" Demi asked.

"I think we need to do what our parents haven't," I said. "Communicate. We need to let the humans know what's going on."

"We could use the emergency alert system," said Tia. "All countries around the world monitor the US's system. Broadcast to one and you broadcast to all."

"And tell them what?" said Loren.

"To pray for mercy or a miracle," I said.

CHAPTER NINETEEN

Clouds gathered overhead, bunching together like an insomniac was punching them into shape to finally fall asleep. The sky crackled, and streams of light rent the atmosphere in two. The flashes of lightning came every other second, replacing the source of light in the darkened sky.

For a moment, I feared the Elohim had come to the surface. But that was absurd. They could do all their dirty work from the safety of the warm core below.

A flash of lightning struck one of the turrets of the Cinderella Castle. The golden spire toppled, knocking into another turret. Fire burst from the center of the castle. The flames grew, licking up the sides of the castle as though an evil stepmother were taking her revenge.

"I'm on it," said Desi. His hands glowed ember-bright as he prepared to do battle with the blaze.

"Gives new meaning to the phrase storming the castle," said Bryn.

Loren gasped, glaring at Bryn. "I was just about to make that joke."

Bryn smirked. "You snooze, you lose."

"Now that was a lame cliché," Loren grumbled.

They both hushed as another current of electricity cracked the sound barrier. This one headed right toward us. The hairs on my arms rose, and sparks raced toward me.

Before impact, something golden streaked before my eyes. Rather, someone golden. Zeus caught the lightning in one palm. With his other hand, he grabbed for another. He gathered the streams of light in his hands and stuffed them into his open mouth.

The air was quiet for a moment. Zuzu looked over his shoulder, eyes flitting to everyone on the ground as though he was counting. He counted me last.

"Thanks," I said.

He winked, ever the incorrigible rake. Then he took off into the sky to capture more snacks of bolts.

I couldn't see Psi and Vivi, but I was certain they were doing all they could to get that hurricane in the Atlantic under control. But none of that would be for anything if we didn't get the greatest danger under control.

On the screens, the newscasters were losing their professional cool. Panic crept into their voices. Fear colored their eyes. The B-roll that flashed over their strained faces was of turbulence and anarchy and chaos as humans sought shelter.

But dotted in amongst the tumult were images of humans helping each other out. The young helped escort the elderly to safety. Mothers handed off their children to strangers so the young would be on higher ground. Emergency personnel risked life and limb to do their duties and protect their fellow citizens.

It warmed my heart. But it wasn't enough. I knew the Elohim, specifically Michael, wouldn't stop at a little bit of water to flush their problem down the drain. They could always send something worse.

They could cause famine, making the soil barren. They could introduce more plagues. Or Eden could just yank the life out of every living thing, if she chose. My idea might be a long shot, but I couldn't think of any other way we could possibly win this fight.

I looked over Hestia's shoulder as she typed on her handheld. "How's it going?"

"It would go faster if I were back in Athens at my super computer with my team of hackers," Tia said. "But I'm making some progress."

If this didn't work, I didn't know what else to do? I stepped back and pressed my face into Zane's chest.

"If I didn't know you well, I'd say you were having doubts," he said.

"I can't figure out a way to win."

"That's never stopped you before. You've chased me to the ends of the earth until I heard your side of arguments to try and prove your point."

"And you didn't always listen to me."

"Not at first. But I did eventually."

Zane pressed a light kiss to my temple. I tilted my head back to accept his kiss on my lips. He was the calm as the storm raged around us.

"I'm in!"

I broke the kiss reluctantly to turn to Tia. Her computer screen held a bunch of code. All that looked familiar to me was the red dot from the video camera that said the feed was live. Great. It was time for my little heart-to-heart with humanity.

"What are you going to say?" asked Loren.

"The truth."

"I've enabled the closed captions to auto translate to all languages," said Tia.

I sat down in front of the camera. My face came into view on the television screen that was broadcasting the news. The Magic Kingdom burned in the background.

"Cut!" Demi called. She raced forward, a deep frown on her face. "Darling, this simply won't do."

First she ran her hands through my hair, but they came away tangled. She gathered my hair in a loose knot at the nape of my neck. Then she produced a small makeup kit and began a touch-up.

"We don't have time, Demi," said Tia.

"There's always time for eyeliner."

Demi tried her best and in the end I looked somewhat TV ready. Finally, it was time. I faced the camera.

"Hello… humanity," I began. "My name is…"

I froze as the red light continued its blinking. After centuries of holding close my anonymity, I was still loath to give my identity up. I'd traipsed across the globe, sneaking in and slipping out of tombs, temples, and dig sites. My identity was precious because I lived long, and I didn't want humans to figure out that I was constantly around. They could only slow me down with their annoying questions or their invasive experiments.

But my secrets were no longer necessary. The world's clock had struck midnight. I was in rags and shoeless, all the magic washed off. Cinderella's castle was burning.

"I'm... Nia. Dr. Nia Rivers, archaeologist."

There, that wasn't so hard. Though my mouth did feel a bit like I'd swallowed dust. Probably all the smoke in the air.

"But I'm more than that. I'm immortal. And a child of God."

Whoa. That sounded awfully pretentious. I looked around at my friends. Loren chewed at her lip, avoiding eye contact like she was the stylish friend and I was her dorky best friend making her look bad. Tres looked pained, like my words were nails on a chalkboard. Zane gave me an encouraging nod.

"Technically, we're all children of God. But I saw her recently and I'm sad to say she is not happy. Oh, yeah, *she*. God's a woman—surprise. I know that's great for women's liberation and all, but there's still the problem of her being pretty pissed at you; all of you."

"Nia, dear," said Demi. "This is prime time television, likely families watching. Maybe you should watch the language."

"Oh, right," I grimaced. "Sorry for saying pissed. Crap, I just said it again. God's not pleased with your behavior over the last two thousand years and she's decided to mete out a huge punishment in the form of genocide."

I looked up for Demi's approval. Unlike Loren she at least looked at me. She gave me a strained smile.

"That hurricane—which is being taken care of by some of my friends—is one example, but it's just the beginning. All the plagues in the Bible, that's about to be rained down on your heads, and I'm not sure we can do anything about it."

"I really don't see how this is helping anything," Bryn stage-whispered. "Tell them to take up arms."

"Shut up," hissed Loren.

"You shut up." Bryn reached for her sword.

Loren reached for hers.

"Ladies." Tres got between the two, placing his back to Loren to contain her, and holding up placating hands to Bryn. The two women backed down reluctantly. Tres nodded for me to continue.

"I just want you to know the truth. I feel like that's the only way to get someone to change their behavior, if they have all the facts and know the consequences. You're all in big trouble. Maybe if you all beg for mercy? She's pretty forgiving, but you guys have been pulling a lot of crap lately. It's been hard for us babysitters to vouch for you. We're trying to buy you some time, but Mom is on her way home and you've left a mess. In the meantime, just get somewhere safe while we try to stall. Don't do anything else to tick her off either. That's all I got."

I looked away from the video screen to my friends. No one cheered my speech. No one clapped at my speech. They all looked pretty hopeless. But no one made any moves to step onto the stage.

Well, Loren made a move to grab the spotlight. Tres reached out and brought her back against him. A salacious grin lit her lips, and from the twinkle in her blue eyes, she was quite happy to stay where she was in his arms.

"Okay, then," I said to the camera. "Good luck, humans."

I had the absurd inclination to put up my thumb.

Luckily, the feed cut first before I could lift my hand. The screen went black. Static filled the silence.

Psi and Vivi, Zuzu and Hera had returned along with Desi.

"Do you think that helped?" I asked.

They all looked from one to the other. Demi picked at the collar of her dress. Zuzu shoved his hands in the pockets of his low-slung jeans. Tia shook her head in the negative. Hera smirked, her eyes glinting with destructive anticipation. I'm sure she was expecting to feast on the souls of damned humans tonight along with her father.

It was unfair. Hera had caused destruction that had cost lives. She clearly hadn't learned her lesson. Still she would neither be punished nor face any consequences, unlike all of humanity.

Back on the wall of flat screens, one solitary television set crackled back to life. The feed came back on with the newscaster speaking into a headset. "I'm being told that the Emergency Alert System has been hacked along with the weather system. We are getting reports that there is no hurricane. I repeat, there is no hurricane."

Weather satellites showed a calm sea, thanks to Psi and Vivi. Even the thunderstorm had died down thanks to Zuzu. And Disney was no longer burning thanks to Desi.

"We are being told that terrorists have taken control over the airwaves. We have pinpointed their location to Disney World. The army has been called in."

No sooner had the words left the reporter's lips did black helicopters fly above. They swarmed the sky like large locusts preparing to deliver a biblical plague. Tanks rolled into the parking lots just beyond the gates to the park.

"No," said Bryn. "I don't think that helped at all."

CHAPTER TWENTY

Tanks crunched over the asphalt and splashed through the puddles of storm water. Civilians at the far end of the lot tried to get out. The military personnel parted the sea of stalled cars and made their way through to form a protective barrier between the kingdom and the human peasants.

Uniformed men and women spilled out of the vehicles. The sinister gleam of assault rifles further darkened the landscape. Barrels arrowed at the most magical place on earth.

"Now we're talking." Bryn drew her sword and braced her feet in the yellow brick of the path we stood upon. Her face tilted up and her nostrils flared. The devilish grin that lifted the corner of her mouth made me question her parentage. "I love the smell of steel and sweat and men. Death is in the air."

This was not going well. I thought I had bought us some time. I had likely only bought us moments from one side of the offensive from below. However, those I was trying to protect had drawn arms.

Zane had said it took a while for my words to persuade him. But he'd known me for millennia. I'd just introduced myself to humans. They had no clue who I was. All they saw was a threat to their families, their way of life, to their own lives, and they were aiming to neutralize it. And right now, we were the prime target.

"Bryn, we can't hurt them," I said.

The corners of the Valkyrie's lips turned down in confusion. "Why not? They're going to hurt us."

"They don't understand the danger they're in, the danger that we're all in. We need to try reason again."

"Okay, you reason with that big barrel of a gun aimed at us. I'm going to bring some heads home to Daddy."

Behind Bryn, Hera lifted a brow in approval. Seriously? What was with daughters of gods and their daddies? What was with all Ishim and their fathers?

The Olympians were forever trying to live down the shadow and shame of their father, Cronus. Bryn and her Valkyrie sisters were forever bringing the souls of the dead to their father, Odin. Zane, Tres, and I all defied our fathers' wishes.

I wondered if all the troubles of the world—this one, the one beneath, and the other realms—could be solved if our dads had simply spent some quality time with us at Disney World in our youth?

With a screeching battle cry, Bryn ran toward the soldiers. Everyone looked to me, as though waiting for my command.

"We can't just stand here," I huffed.

"All right," said Desi. "But are we stopping the blood-thirsty Valkyrie with a magical sword of light? Or are we attacking the humans with the guns and missiles?"

I opened my mouth. Then I shut it. Precious seconds ticked away in my indecisiveness. The muffled grumbles and screams said it was too late. Bryn had reached the army.

Bryn slowed her charging run to a moderate canter. Confusion and disappointment colored her face as one by one the army of men and women fell like plastic toys.

A body was thrown into the air. Its gun fired into the sky, its muzzle sparking like fireworks. Another body was thrown to the side. And yet another yanked from one of the Humvees and discarded.

The soldiers faced away from us, trying to meet the threat. It was amongst them, not coming from our side.

The deep growl of a large feline predator rumbled low. I saw a flash of fur. The flash of an eye. The glint of fang.

"Are those wolves?" asked Demi.

"No, I think it's a jaguar," said Tia.

Shots rang out, but the pride of shifters quickly pounced on the military, knocking the soldiers unconscious or just impotent. The animal threat was unexpected, but the humans weren't outfoxed completely.

The leader of the band of misguided human protectors called for the soldiers to close ranks. Unfortunately, he didn't check his flank first.

Under the dark of night, flashes of gray and white came up on the other side of the humans. The wolves plowed through the remaining rows of humans with ease. Knocked them down to the ground. Disabused them of their weapons. Made them add to the puddles of storm water with tears and other fluids.

Out of the fray, a woman emerged. Two women. Walking side by side. Bare from head to toe after their change. Boobs pointed up proud in all their royal glory.

"Skye, Skully?" I raced to the gates to meet them, embracing their naked flesh in my arms. "What are you doing here?"

"Us?" said Skye. "You're one to talk." She frowned at me and then spotted Zane in the crowd and growled at him.

"After you two *died*"—Skully looked accusingly at me—"the Deadbeats said to be here at this day and time if we cared to collect you."

The Deadbeats? She meant her fathers: Hunahpú and Xbalanqué, the God Twins.

"They knew?" said Zane. "Back as far as the Serpent Mound, they knew exactly what would happen. And they let it happen."

Anger was plain on Zane's face. But I was uncertain. The God Twins were tricky. If they knew what was going to happen, and they didn't warn us against it, they had a reason for letting this all play out. What game were they playing?

Another male made his way onto the scene. No, not one male, two. One more delectable than the other.

I tried to tear my eyes away. Really, I did. But a girl was entitled to look.

Zane, who never showed an ounce of jealousy, let out a gruff sound as the Mohegan twins strode forward in all their delicious, naked, delicious, tan… did I say delicious?… glory. Their dark curtains of locks blew in the windless night. Their muscles rippled as they flexed, glistening with the sweat they'd just broke saving our asses.

"More are coming," said Chak as he and his brother, Saka, came to stand before us.

No one answered. No one moved. Well, the men all shifted in annoyance. The women fidgeted and fanned themselves and sighed.

"Hello," said Loren, Bryn, and Demi. Hera cocked her head to the side. Tia tugged at the collar of her prim business shirt. Even Vivi stared with wide eyes.

"We'll need to take cover," said Saka. "We weren't able to get into the tank. That missile is still in play."

"You don't think they'd fire on Disney World," said Tres. "It's a national treasure."

In response, the gravel crunched as the tank

maneuvered into place. It turned on its tracks to aim the long barrel at the Magical Kingdom. Well, that answered that question.

"We have to get out of here," I said.

"I know a place that's impenetrable," Loren said. "I just need to tap into a ley line. There's enough energy here somewhere. I can feel it."

Loren closed her eyes and held out her hands. She took a couple of tentative steps like a blind woman without her cane. But then her steps picked up.

I motioned for everyone to follow her. Zane and Tres, Bryn, the Olympians, the Balam and the Mohegan all crowded around the divining witch. She led us to Fantasy Land and the small castle there.

"Really?" I said. "Here?"

"Children's wishes are as potent as prayers," Loren said.

Ley lines existed on places of great importance to humans. Places where they showed devotion and care. We stood outside of the It's a Small World ride.

My bestie shut her eyes again. She held out her hands and began to chant. The tank still crunched in the distance.

"Loren?"

"Hush," she warned. A small light emitted from her hand, making a tiny circle of a portal. Not enough to fit a single body through.

A loud bang split the air. The odious smell of chemicals burned my nose. But even more disturbing was the bright blaze of light arrowing toward us.

"Loren!"

Loren continued her chant, unhurried, her voice barely above a whisper. With barely a second to spare, the small window of energy opened into a large door.

We all raced through. The last wolf's paw crossed the threshold when the explosive crashed into the castle. The wolf yipped as a few flames tugged at its tail. Loren clasped her hands together and the hole closed into darkness.

Silence rang out, but the ringing of the explosion still shrouded us. Loren grinned at me, holding up her hand for a high five.

"Look at you." I slapped her palm.

"Learned a couple of new tricks since you've been away." She grinned.

"Where are we?" someone asked. I'm not sure who. Our small band had grown to a medium-size force. But it was about to get larger.

"You're in my house."

I grimaced at the deep growl. It didn't make me squirm like the growl of the Mohegan Twins. It got my hackles up and made me yearn for a blade.

"Hey, Artie," I said.

I turned to see not only his big barrel of a medieval chest, but also Sir Lance and Sir Tristan as well.

"Are we in Camelot?" I asked Loren.

"No," Lance answered. "You're still in Florida. This is one of our strongholds."

"How did you guys know to come here?" I asked.

"Igraine," said Tristan.

It was the only word needed. I wished the old witch were here now. She gave the best hugs, and I needed one since my dad was trying to kill me. Or at the least, he was complacent in my demise.

"What have you done?" Arthur said.

I opened my mouth to respond. But for once in my life it wasn't me his ire was cast upon. He glared at Loren.

"I told you not to trifle with a god," he said. "'Loren, do not steal Odin's hammer,' I said. 'Loren, do not go to the Garden.' And what do you do?"

"This is not my fault," said Loren. "This was already in play when I got there."

"She made it worse," volunteered Bryn.

"And you bring wolves and Greeks and fae into a castle?" said Arthur.

"We're all on the same side," I said.

"Against who?" said Arthur. "Who's on the other side? Would that be God?"

"No, not precisely," I hedged. "It would be God and her angels."

Arthur shook his head. "What did you steal now?"

"I didn't steal anything," I said. "I'm trying to save the world. That's in the knights' job description, right?"

Arthur fingered the scabbard of his sword. "What do you need?"

"I don't know. All we've been doing so far is running. First from Eden and the Elohim, then from the human military."

We'd been caught in the middle. Which was funny, because we all were in the middle of this war. We were children of gods, or somehow touched by gods. But we made our homes on the surface, surrounded by humans.

It was time to take a stand. But where? How?

"Everyone," said Lance. "I think you need to come and see this."

Lance stood at the window of the castle. I marched over to him. We were up high in a turret. It gave us a clear view of the sky.

From the sky, fire and brimstone rained down like meteors. But they weren't meteors. They were Elohim. They were here. They were coming to the surface and headed toward the amusement park.

CHAPTER TWENTY-ONE

We came out the front doors of the medieval castle in the heart of Orlando. The Arthurian stronghold was a true brick-and-mortar castle, but the front was a luxury hotel. An exclusive luxury hotel where no mere mortal had ever been admitted.

Once the drawbridge was raised, we were confronted with a scene out of a dystopian novel. The streets of Orlando were cluttered with immobile cars. There wasn't a soul about in the darkness. Even nearby homes were cast in shadows.

With the ley line's doorway into the park blown to bits, thanks to the military, we headed back to the park on foot. Not all of us walked on two feet.

The shifters ran on four legs. Loren tried to

climb on Saka's back, but Tres took one arm and Arthur another and hefted her onto a magical steed from the castle's stables. The rest of us bipeds road on horseback. Those with other godly attributes, like the ability to harness fire, water, or lightning, sailed through the air on said elements.

"It's like the Avengers assembled," said Loren. There was a light in her eyes as she claimed the title for us all.

I tried not to laugh as we headed back into a battle that I had no idea how it would end. But I giggled despite myself. A little levity couldn't hurt this moment.

Beside her, Tres gave her the exact same look, trying but failing not to laugh. The corner of his mouth kicked into a rare grin. He caught me looking and averted his gaze from my best friend, his natural brooding scowl affixed firmly back in place.

"I've seen that one. There's only one woman in that film," said Bryn. She rode in front of us. Her dark tresses trailed behind her like a personal wind had assigned itself to her and kept her shining face in the spotlight. "And that woman, the Russian one, she's a human. She doesn't have any powers outside of the ability to wrap a man between her thighs. I prefer the Justice League, myself. Much more pro female."

Loren scowled and looked to me for backup.

"She has a point," I said.

"I'm not talking about the film," Loren said. "I'm talking about the comics. And DC Comics mainly has male cast-offs of females like Batgirl, Hawkgirl, the Wasp, and freakin' She Hulk."

"She Hulk was an embarrassment," said Bryn, "but they also have Wonder Woman."

Loren opened her mouth to protest. Then she closed it and tilted her head. Both Loren and Bryn tilted their heads as though weighing this last piece of evidence of an Amazonian, sword-wielding princess, before coming to a mutual conclusion. Loren ceded the battle. All was quiet for a few moments until we turned the corner.

We came back to the park. The bottleneck to the highway had cleared, and all the families that had been enjoying the park that day had evacuated. All that remained was the military. As predicted, they'd called for backup.

More tanks had rolled in. More troops replaced those who'd fallen. Many of the fallen were on their feet again.

I had hoped that they might stand down now

that they saw beings of light rain down from the sky. No such luck. Like cockroaches, they were. Stomp on them, but they rise again, bringing their friends for a taste of the danger.

A chorus of guns cocking sounded in the night. A few weapons clattered to the ground as the Balam Queens and the Mohegan Twins amidst their packs took on human forms before the soldiers' eyes.

A single shot rang out. But a bullet wasn't much to most of us. It was easily dodged, and then it was our turn to keep the peace.

Loren raised her hands, and with her powers, she lifted the muzzles off the front row of guns. If they wanted to pull the triggers, the soldiers would shoot birds. Psi and Vivi sent water to collect weapons from the remaining soldiers. I was pretty sure we had their attention now.

"Remember us?" I asked.

The tank clanked and whirred as the turret turned toward us. Desi raised his hand, and the green of the painted metal turned a rusted red as it heated.

A man oozing the authority of one with a large number of bars and stars popped out of the tank and climbed down. I assumed he was in charge.

"Hear me now," I said to the advancing human

leader. "Not a single one of your soldiers is dead, and you can see that was our choice."

The man was red-faced as he halted in front of me. He was brave, I'll give him that. I just hoped he had ears large enough to listen.

"You're no terrorists," he said. "I'm not sure you're human. What in god's name are you?"

"It doesn't matter." I pointed to the Elohim advancing from the gates of the park. "Those are the real bad guys. And they will not extend you the same courtesy we have. In fact, they've come here with the express purpose to eradicate humankind."

In the crowd of soldiers, a few raised a cross to their lips. A few others made the sign of the cross over their hearts. And I swore I heard the beginning of a psalm about the shadow of the valley of death.

I refrained from shaking my head. If only they knew what shadow was about to fall over them. I turned my attention back to the military leader. "I'm going to offer you some advice, and I hope you'll take it. Stay out of this."

He looked around at the insurmountable odds. He looked at the Ishim, wolves, jaguars, knights in armor, gods who controlled the elements. Then he looked beyond us at the approaching Elohim.

They were all in skins, but their light was no

match for the flesh. It shone through, bright as a fluorescent light. It was clear they weren't human. That they were something else. A few humans correctly guessed: angels.

"Sorry, ma'am," the leader said. "Afraid I can't do that. Not in my blood to turn tail. I've got a family to fight for. So do all these soldiers. We have family, friends, country... hell, humankind to fight for."

Behind him, the men and women, who were divested of their weapons, still stood ready to defend those they'd sworn to protect.

"You're a good man," I said.

"I still don't know who or what you are." He eyed me with a level gaze. "But we'll stand with you."

"Ishim," said a voice as deep as a drum. My father stood only feet away from me. His gaze was on me as he spoke to us all. "Move out of harm's way."

"We're not the ones doing harm." Zane moved in front of me. He addressed my father, but his gaze was on his own sire.

"The time of humans is up," said Michael. "You children can move or face the same consequences."

Instead of moving, the Ishim all gathered in a line. Tres stood beside his brother.

"So be it," said Michael.

"You'd kill your own sons?" asked Loren. "That's cold-blooded. But then you have no blood, so…"

Not a single crease of emotion touched Michael's eye. "I've had many sons. I'll have more."

Gabriel turned his head almost imperceptibly toward Michael. So did a few other angels, not a majority. That's when I saw who all this army of light was comprised of. There were many Elohim whose faces I didn't recognize. But I knew a few.

Off to the side, Rhea clutched Cronus with one hand. Cronus's nose was up in the air, his mouth hanging wide like a dog sniffing a bone. His eyes were glued to the army of humans just within his hungry reach.

The God Twins looked on with their typical amusement. They also eyed the humans in uniform, likely searching out any women with Native American blood to toy with before, during, or maybe even after this trial was over.

"Hey, Dads," said Chak.

The twins gave their offspring a fleeting glance and a slight nod of acknowledgement.

"You think you're fighting for all of creation," I said to Michael. "But you're not. You're fighting for yourself."

"Precisely," said Michael. "If we allow these ill

breeds to continue to exist and infest the surface, it will mean the end of creation."

"But that's just it," I said. I waved my empty hands for emphasis. Arthur had offered me the use of a sword, but I had declined. This battle wouldn't be won with weapons of steel. Our only chance was words.

"They're not going backwards. None of us are. We're the ones going forward. Evolution isn't going backward. It's gone beyond you and you can't stand it. You're like someone's grandpa who can't work a cell phone. You can't blow up the world for that, because you've been left behind."

"Preach the truth, sister," Loren shouted.

I opened my empty hands toward Michael. Thought better of it and faced my own father. "Let us show you how it works, all these emotions and feelings. The ability to connect even though you're covered in flesh. You might like it."

Gabriel's eye twitched. Rhea teared up. I ignored the God Twins; their comments, if they said any, were likely lewd and sexual.

"Enough of this," said Michael.

"No," I said. "Enough of you. You've tried to destroy everything that breathes life. It's not creation that's the problem. It's you. You're the one who can't change. You can't evolve."

"There's no need."

For a second, I thought maybe I was wrong. Michael's lip curled into a snarl. Anger lit his eyes. So, he did feel. It was just burning, ugly feelings.

"We were born perfect," he said.

"Ego much?"

Michael sniffed. His eyes narrowed on me. His hands clenched into fists and a dark light grew there. He stepped toward me. A crowd gathered at my back, and I knew my friends and family were there.

Before Michael could take that first step, Gabriel put out his hand.

Michael glared at Gabriel. Silent communication passed between the two. Then Gabriel gave us his back and walked backward. Toward us.

My dad crossed an imaginary line in the asphalt of the parking lot. Michael watched him go. It took much longer for the Elohim to comprehend exactly what was happening. By then, it was too late.

Other Elohim followed Gabriel across the divide. Rhea. Followed by Cronus, on his leash. Rhea dropped the leash when Hera flew into her father's arms, tethering him with her forbidden love.

Others crossed, Elohim I didn't know. And two I

did. The God Twins stood at the back of the line, closest to the human army. Their children just rolled their eyes and mouthed *deadbeats*.

Our enhanced army faced off against Michael and his smaller number of Elohim. The odds were a bit more even now, and I felt the first true pangs of hope. Until…

Fire lit the sky. Eden streaked across the horizon on a dragon. The odds had swayed out of our favor once more.

CHAPTER TWENTY-TWO

The dragon's dark wings stretched behind Eden like a cape. She wasn't clothed. Flesh covered her bright essence. In the waning moonlight, her light cast a reddish glow, a living fire riding in the night.

Some of the soldiers fell to their knees at the sight. Their heavy boots kicked up rocks as they prostrated themselves. Others, brawny men with visible battle scars, openly wept. Women tilted up their heads and wailed in various languages for their savior.

"Children of the Earth," said Eden, "hear me."

She was far away from us, up in the sky, but her words touched my ears. They touched my soul. She spoke not only in every tongue known to man, she also called out telepathically to the flora and fauna that inhabited this womb of a rock.

"I am your Lord God. I know my existence has been doubted by many of you. But I assure you, I am no figment. I am quite alive. I have been here since the dawn of time."

A monitor in one of the jeeps came to life. I hadn't noticed before because the screen had been dark. Now it filled with Eden and the dragon, as much as the drone camera could chase after them and keep the two mystical creatures in its viewfinder.

"I am indeed omniscient, with knowledge of every action that has taken place on this rock. I am omnipotent with unlimited power. I am omnipresent as my essence is evident in every blade of grass to every creature that breathes."

Michael made a grinding sound, his jaw clenched as though he was gnashing his teeth. His features were pinched as his gaze stayed trained on Eden. For a being who never showed emotion, he was clearly not happy to see her.

Up in the sky, the dragon reared up. The claws at the tips of its wings framed its sinewy body. Eden's bald head formed its crown as she continued her sermon.

"You have spent your time worshipping me when

all I asked was for your excellence. But you have not excelled. You have desecrated my house, profaned my name, and destroyed much of my creation. I am not pleased."

The few humans who had stood stoic under this divine assault now quivered in their boots. The Ishim even looked chastised. Arthur's head hung low, even though his people had done no such thing. He was likely thrashing himself internally that he hadn't done enough. The suck-up.

"I have sent warning after warning of my displeasure. I have sent flood waters. I have sent disease and pestilence. But you have not heeded my instruction, and for that I called for the eradication of your kind."

Pandemonium set in on those words. The humans of the army ran for cover. These were the trained professionals. I could only imagine what everyday civilians across the globe were doing. I looked around for the commander, but I couldn't find him anywhere in the crowd. So much for sticking up for family and mankind.

"But I realize that I have been mistaken."

Too late. Her words had incited the worst response in humanity. Then I spotted the commander. He was climbing into the tank.

"I should have used my words. I should have come to the surface and scolded you face to face to make you mind your manners. I've been a bad mother."

Beside me, Bryn made a sound that was partly *duh* and *pfft* put together. I couldn't take the moment to stand in solidarity with my fellow neglected Ishim. I had to get to that tank before the commander did something god-awful.

"Still," Eden continued, "you have been a bunch of spoiled brats and you do need to be taught to mind. All of you."

As I moved through the crowd of humans, Eden narrowed her gaze down below. I wished I could see the look on Michael's face as he was finally called to the carpet.

What had made Eden finally see the errors of her ways? The rebellion of her own children? Maybe the sight of the Elohim staring at each other from across a divide. None of it would matter if I didn't get to the tank.

I leapt over a few soldiers crowding the tank. As I ran, a gun cocked. A bullet would have slowed me down in my past life. With my skin so thin, it might just send me back to the core, and then who would stand up for these humans?

But the trigger never clicked. The bullet never flew. An ancient curse was spoken, a thud, and then the clink of metal on metal, like a sword meeting a gun.

Behind me, my friends, the family I had chosen, had my back. Like always. They'd taken down whatever human had been told to protect the tank and the commander. But it was too late.

The turret of the tank creaked. It turned until it aimed at Eden, clothed in human flesh, with glowing red skin, seated on a flying serpent with horns.

Crap.

Damn humans. Damn them and their misinterpretations and misunderstandings. Damn them and their fallacies and their fears. Damn them for their emotional hearts and overactive imaginations.

The blast shook me to my core, my words of warning catching in my throat.

The stream of explosive fire arrowed directly toward Eden—like a heat-seeking missile. She was made of light. Even if she tried to outrun it, it would've easily found her.

Eden didn't run. She saw it. Her head cocked like a bird as she watched it.

Time slowed down. My throat cleared. My vision clouded.

Eden reached out, and her body lifted off the dragon. The blast arrowed straight for her hand, which happened to be at the center of her chest.

A brilliant array of color exploded. It rivaled what she'd shown me of her own birth, with reds and yellows and sparks. But as the colors died down, the night went dark again. Nothing remained in the spot where Eden had been.

The silence was deafening. The Elohim and Ishim gasped in disbelief. The humans cheered in victory; a few of the devout ones wailed.

God was dead.

CHAPTER TWENTY-THREE

h my god.

God was dead.

An eerie silence fell over the three armies: the humans, the Ishim, and the Elohim. The dark night lit up as the dragon fell from the sky. It spread its wings at the last minute and broke its landing. But hit the ground with enough force that wobbled everyone. Even a few of the Elohim lost their footing at the great animal's landing.

But not all of them.

Michael turned his face up to the empty sky where Eden had hovered. The space was black now where light had shown. A grin slit his cruel face.

From the first moment I'd seen him, he had looked expressionless. But those without expression, those who caused others pain without care, those who could not understand the stress they caused another living soul, those beings were true psychopaths. And Michael had to be the most psychotic being that had ever lived.

Humans had believed the devil to live below the surface of the earth. I now knew they were right. But it wasn't their souls the fiend was interested in. It was their absence. And now nothing stood in his way.

Michael lifted his hand and aimed. A fireball shot out of his hand. The ball of light aimed right at the tank.

I had only a second to move out of harm's way. Before I could decide which direction to go, I hurtled into the air.

I landed far away in Zane's arms. He crouched low as his legs took the impact of striking the ground from a great distance.

Then he shielded my face as a thick liquid rained down. Blood. Blood from the humans who didn't get out of the way in time. But not only blood.

Metal pieces from the tank ruptured, crashing into other humans, spraying not only parts of the tank but body parts. The iron in both the metal and the blood stung my nose.

Zane placed me back on my feet when the rain stopped. The remaining soldiers scrambled for their weapons, for cover, for a safety that no longer existed for them. The Ishim and Elohim who had stood in front of the army for their protection still stared into the night sky, still shell-shocked at our collective loss. No one stood in Michael's way.

"You have one chance only," said Michael. "Lay down your weapons and submit. Perhaps I will show leniency to a few dozen of mankind."

"Leniency?" I shouted into the rising panic of the humans, the crushing sorrow of the light beings and their halfling children. "Like you did the dragons? Or perhaps the kindness you showed the fae that had them flee to another realm to be away from you?"

I made my way toward the god of darkness. No one stopped me. But my friends rallied enough to gather at my back as I stood before Michael.

"You don't want anything to flourish," I said. "You'll shove everything down so you can rise above."

"You're wrong." Michael smiled, and I was sorry to see it. The contortions of his face made the hair on the back of my neck flatten to escape his notice. "I was always above. Everything that has come since is vermin under my feet."

"You don't want peace," I said. "You need adversity to survive. You're the worst type of being."

He raised his hand to me. I prepared to have my flesh rent in two, my light yanked from my body, for disease to take hold of me and never let me go for an eternity. But that didn't happen.

Zane pulled me into his strong arms. My best friend stepped to my side. Tres stood behind me. My father stepped in front of us all.

In the face of all this adversity, Michael didn't lower his hands. They glowed an angry red in the face of this rebellion. I braced for impact.

Still, it didn't come.

Michael's hand was raised, a bright light still burning in the center of his palm. The same light burned in the center of my father's palm. But the flames didn't grow. Neither of them moved.

Zane's arms remained around me. His face was a fierce, immovable mask.

Everyone, everything around me was frozen.

No. Not frozen. There was movement, but they all moved slowly, as if time had slowed down.

In the stillness of the frozen moment, a light shone up on a hill. It came from inside the park. It came from the last remaining turret of the Cinderella Castle.

I walked through a sea of snail-paced people as God stretched out this moment in time. I went back through the gates of Disney World.

Eden sat on the statue of Walt Disney and Mickey Mouse. Against all odds, the statue was unharmed. She sat on Disney's right shoulder, looking down at where the creator held his creation's hand.

I hefted myself up to Disney's other shoulder. We sat in silence for a moment. I had no idea what to say, but I knew she wanted to say something to me— I was the only other living thing not slogging through time in slo-mo.

"I remember making these," Eden finally said.

She focused on Mickey. I didn't think she meant that she'd made the statue.

"I made them around the same time that I made the dragons. I've always thought beings should exist in both large forms and small." She ran a hand over Mickey's metallic ear. "And they're still here. Though I don't remember them evolving to bipeds."

"They haven't," I said. "It's just a bit of imagination. Humans like to give animals personalities and feelings. They call it anthropomorphizing."

"Hmmm." Eden brought her hand back into her

lap. Then she looked out at the frozen melee before us. "This is not what I intended. This is not what I designed."

Her creations aimed violence and vengeance at one another. The divided Elohim. The rebellious Ishim. The frightened humans.

"I was born out of adversity," Eden said. "All my life I've strived toward harmony. I'm not naive enough to think there would be no strife and struggle in progression. Iron sharpens iron. Diamonds are forged through pressure. But diamonds don't seek to crush each other like my creations do.

"Life is a miracle. I know that. I'm a miracle. I fought to stay alive. I waited so long for something else to be born. I thought I would be the only one that would have to fight. Yet every few centuries, sometimes more frequently, my creations wage wars in my name when I don't want them to. Never asked them to. But it always comes to this. It seems life cannot exist without struggle. Maybe it was all a mistake."

"What do you mean?" I asked.

"Maybe I was a mistake. And if I was a mistake..."

"Then all of creation is a mistake."

Seriously? God was having a crisis of faith right

now. In the distance, I spied Zane's statuesque body. He had his arms up as though he still held me. Tres had his brother's back. The two had been through strife for centuries, but they found a way back together.

Loren and I had begun in adversity. But now, we would've died for each other. Almost had a couple of times.

Demi and I had fallen out but come back together. I could say the same for each of my friends. We made mistakes. But when we eventually addressed our error of ways, we were able to make the relationships stronger even with the mishap that had torn us apart.

"When Zane makes a mistake in his art," I said, "he incorporates it in his design. He never erases. There's beauty in every line, even the ones that steer him off his original course."

Eden cocked her head in that thoughtful way of hers. "I do like to combine things."

"Like the platypus?"

She turned to me. "What's wrong with the platypus?"

"Oh, nothing," I said. "When we forget our mistakes, when we forget the past, we're doomed to repeat it. The dinosaurs. The fae. Now humans."

"I don't forget anything. I know all these things. I just stopped paying attention."

I didn't respond.

"Go on," she said. "Say it."

"I... *told you so*."

I stared into the eyes of God. Her bright orbs weren't empty, fathomless pools of stillness. They were a raging inferno of sorrow and resignation.

"I've been a bad mother," she said.

I turned away from her and looked at anything else. Unfortunately, there was nothing to look at, as everything was still in super-slow motion.

"I still don't like that word," she said. "Mother. It's a tad harsh on the ears."

Eden touched the pointy tip of her ear. Then she sighed, turning her attention to the delayed mess that needed her motherly attention.

"What are you going to do?" I asked.

"Discipline my children. I've spared the rod too long. I now admit it: my children are spoiled."

CHAPTER TWENTY-FOUR

*E*den and I made our way down from the statue of the creator and the figment of his imagination. We walked the silent streets of Disney World. Fireflies hung in the air, their tails glowing bright.

Upon closer inspection it was clear to see that each fly pursued another of its species. The lightning bugs were cannibals, and would either mate or snack on the glowing tails of its partner, depending which urge took it most strongly.

We passed through the gates of the amusement park and came up on the back end of the Elohim siding with Michael. Eden sighed as she stood before the living statue of one of her first creations.

Her bright eyes dimmed as she took in Michael's carnivorous sneer as he faced off against Gabriel.

"I failed you most of all, haven't I?" She cocked her head at Michael.

She was met with a steely gaze in this stretched moment as Michael focused on the target of his ire.

"I'm going to dismantle that horrible human weapon and then I'll be back to clean up this mess," she said.

Eden began to fade away, but I reached out to her.

"Eden, can you give me a moment with him?" I pointed across the divide to the man in question. "There's something I want to say to him before this is over."

Eden cocked her head in that birdlike fashion. "Are you sure you want that one? I rather fancy the other one."

"Yes. I've made my choice. I'm sure."

Eden didn't reach out to touch his broad shoulders. She blinked her bright eyes, and, as though waking from a dream, he stumbled forward. He wasn't looking at me. His gaze was latched onto Loren. His shoulder was in line with Zane.

Tres looked around in confusion a moment at

the stasis of his surroundings before his gaze landed on me.

"Hey," I said when I had his attention.

"Nia?" said Tres. His hands were still up in a defensive position. He lowered one arm with uncertainty. "What's going on?"

"Oh, Eden is disarming the humans and then she's gonna come back and handle this little situation here with the Elohim."

Tres lowered his other arm even slower. "She's alive?"

"Well, she is God."

"So…" He looked around at the freeze-framed scene again. "Our work here is done?"

"Yeah, everything's good." I pressed my lips together in a slight grimace, then forged ahead. "Listen, I just wanted a quick chat with you before time starts up again."

"Okay." Tres blinked at me. He scratched at his temple. Then he put his hands in his pockets. "What's up?"

"Things have just been so crazy the last couple of days, or hours, or however long it's been, I'm not sure with the whole above the core and below the core time differences, and we haven't had a chance to talk."

I was babbling. And the silence stretched on. What the hell was wrong with me that it was difficult to talk to him? We'd known each other for millennia. Maybe that was the problem. We knew each other.

"Nia?" he said. "I'm not sure how time is working now, but I'm sure we don't have a whole lot of it left before God finishes whatever she's doing to make the world safe. What do you want to talk about?"

"Right. Speaking of Eden, I was just talking to her about rivalry and making mistakes and forgiveness."

"Okay."

"It's just…"

"It's just what, *Theta*?"

Tres reached out to me. His touch was so familiar, such a comfort. Had his touch always been this comforting? Had his voice always set me at ease?

It had. I was suddenly so sure. The time we'd been at each other's throats, when we'd been enemies and not friends, when desire or guilt or shame had clouded our gazes, that had been a brief history of our time together. This was the natural state for the two of us.

"It's just that I want us to be good too," I said. "You and I got back into a good place. And it looks like you and Zane are on the mend. I just wanted to make sure we're okay too."

Tres smiled, eyes soft as he regarded me. He reached out again, wrapping his fingers around my bicep. It wasn't proprietary. It wasn't filled with heat. It was the most natural thing in the world.

"We're fine, Nia."

"Good." I sighed. "We've had such a torrid past. Friends, at each other's throats, at each other in different ways, enemies, dating, and now…"

"And now…" Tres glanced to where Zane stood frozen. "I'm assuming you're back in a serious, committed relationship?"

"Yes."

"And for good this time?"

My brows furrowed. The hairs above my eyes weren't sure they liked his tone. I wasn't sure I liked his tone, but I nodded.

"And your affections are beyond my reach?"

I yanked my arm out of his friendly hold. "They were beyond your reach before, and that didn't stop you from chasing me."

Tres's amiable grin slipped. He pointed his index finger at me. "You let me catch you."

We glared at each other. This was all too familiar. So ridiculously familiar that we both burst out laughing. Standing there in the center of a paused apocalypse.

"I don't want to do this," I said. "I don't want us to be enemies again."

"That's not going to happen. It wasn't necessarily your affection I was after."

We both turned again to Zane. He stood frozen, embracing me even though I wasn't there. Unaware that he was the current topic of conversation.

"He's my brother." Tres said. "And you took him away. Then he couldn't take his eyes off you. I'm competitive."

"So, you admit you chased me," I said.

"And caught you, I might add."

I grinned, conceding the point.

"But I know I won't have that with you," he said. "It was different with us. What the two of you have is unique. It can only be between the two of you."

"We could share him."

"Oh, you don't have a choice." Tres grinned. "I've come to realize exactly how important family is recently."

"Do we get to share you?" I asked.

"Absolutely." Then he frowned. "Maybe separately at first. It is kinda weird right now. Our immediate past." He motioned between us. "And our distant past." He motioned between himself and Zane.

"Yeah. You're right."

"So...?"

"So, we're good?"

Tres's mouth split into a slow grin. Then he opened his arms. "Yeah. We're good."

I came into his arms. "I do love you, you know."

"I know. I've always known. Just as I've always known that it would always be the two of you. I was so angry for years, centuries, because I wanted something like that for myself. I tried to take it from him. What I didn't realize is that I'd have to take it from you too. I can build things people worship, things people want for all time, but no one has ever wanted me that way."

I pulled away and looked into his eyes. There was a sadness there I'd never seen before. "She's out there. The woman who'll love you that way. I just know it."

His downcast eyes focused hard on the ground, as though he didn't dare look up.

"Maybe," Tres said.

And then, as though he couldn't help himself, his gaze flicked past me, past Zane, to someone else.

Before I could follow the trajectory we were interrupted.

"Are you two finished with your little tête-à-tête?" asked Eden. "That's French. I like the French language, so soft and delicate on the ears."

"Yeah," I said. "We're good."

"We're good," Tres confirmed.

I let go of Tres and slipped back into Zane's arms. But instead of taking my former position with him at my back, I faced him.

There had been a time when I'd have to wait days, months to see him. There'd been a time when we had to fight technology just to speak to one another. Those days were over. I could hold onto him forever now without getting sick or disconnected or forgetful. So long as we made trips down to the core to shed our worldly skin, he would be mine forever.

I pressed my lips to his. Even though he was frozen, his heat, his warmth, the sense of forever in this stretched moment touched me. Tres was right. This was unique, the thing between Zane and me.

Time stopped again as Eden released her hold on the moment. Zane startled as I pressed our lips together. He instinctively brought me to him in a protective hold. But there was no longer any danger. He didn't know and so he pulled me closer.

"We're fine," I said. "All is well."

A blast came behind Zane as the tank exploded. When it did, not a single human remained in the street. I hadn't watched Eden remove them all, but she had.

A cry of pain over my shoulder followed the blast. Zane switched our positions, placing me behind him.

Michael kneeled before Eden. The Elohim behind him were also on their knees, but they did it by choice. Eden had a hold on Michael, a hold he fought against and lost.

"Stop fighting," she said. "It's so unnecessary."

"They'll be the end of us all," said Michael.

"If they are, then it's my fault. They're my responsibility. You all are."

Eden looked out at the gathered Elohim on each side. She took in each of the Ishim. Then her gaze turned to the human witch and knights, as well, and she nodded with approval.

Her gaze found Michael's once more. "I chose well. You led a third of the Elohim away from me. That takes true leadership."

Michael bristled. I doubt he cared for the praise, especially seeing that his advancement had failed.

"Your vision was skewed," said Eden. "You were trying to take us backward. Back to a world without a form. Back to the void. It's you who have rebelled and become an adversary."

Eden's eyes filled with the soft, pale, flooded light of sorrow. And finally, Michael hung his head. Whether from guilt at what he had attempted or sorrow for not succeeding, I didn't know. I didn't particularly care.

"We'll talk when we get home and I give you your punishment," Eden said.

"Oooh," Bryn sing-songed. "You're in trouble." Her mother hushed her with a stern look.

"For now, I'll put enmity between you and humanity." Eden set her hand on Michael's shoulder and shoved him downward. The earth beneath his knees opened and swallowed him whole.

"He should've been torn apart," muttered Bryn. "I should be carting his soul back to the Halls of Valhalla."

"Bryn," said Eden, "we don't kill everything that irritates or disagrees with us. That was Michael's folly. That's what communication is for."

Bryn snorted in disbelief.

Eden turned to her daughter with a raised brow. That arched brow was the universal, unspoken mom language of *Do not argue with me out in public, missy.* Bryn held her tongue.

Eden chewed her lip like she was choosing her words carefully. "I haven't done very much with you and your sisters in a while, have I?"

Bryn opened her mouth. By the look on her face, I got the feeling she was about to take issue with that *a while* and replace it with *at all*. But the Valkyrie's lips curved in a different direction -in the downward direction of shut.

"That changes now," said Eden. "Run home and tell your father I'm taking my girls for a mother-daughter weekend."

Bryn's eyes lit up. She reached for her mother, paused, then moved forward with her initial motion, flinging her arms around her. Eden's large eyes widened slightly. She raised a hand and patted Bryn awkwardly on the back before Bryn let her go and took off.

Eden faced me. "How long is a weekend exactly?"

"It's two days."

Eden considered that and then nodded.

She faced the rest of the Elohim.

"I'm going to pay better attention to everyone." But then she thought about it. "Well, there are an awful lot of you. Let me amend that. I think I'll delegate better. Perhaps I'll write down the instructions myself this time. You'll help me with that, won't you, Nia?"

CHAPTER TWENTY-FIVE

Thump! Thump!
Everyone jerked and covered their ears as Eden flicked her finger on the microphone.

"Is this thing on?" she asked.

Screech. Garble garble.

Eden reared back. Her big eyes flashed fire-bright. Her palms filled with golden heat as she eyed the technology with suspicion and disdain.

Hestia hooked up the last connection of the live feed to broadcast across the entire planet. Now everyone would have the message from God, direct from her lips. The Greek goddess had also set up a share site on the internet so the message would last for all lifetimes, or as long as the World Wide Web stayed intact.

The television screen went from black to bright white light. Eden was so bright you couldn't exactly see her face. She looked more like a figure in the spotlight.

The park remained empty, except for the few Elohim who remained. Most had returned to the core, namely Michael's contingent, awaiting their punishment once Eden was done with her directive to the creation above ground.

The parking lot where the short-lived battle for humanity—or against humanity, depending upon which side you were on—remained empty as well, though a few headlights and cellphone cameras flickered. No one dared come closer to the action with all the abandoned military vehicles in the way. I still had no idea where Eden had deposited the army.

"Now, children," Eden began. "Let's try this again."

She paused and looked around at those who remained by her side. Well, we weren't by her side. We were in front of her or behind her. Out of the way, but close by in case she needed a hand with the alien tech.

Only the Elohim who were parents and their children remained on the surface. Rhea and Cronus gathered around their children. All but Hera cast a wary eye on their father. Hunahpú and Xbalanqué were surrounded by their pack, some on human legs, others on four.

Gabriel stood to the side watching the proceedings, his attention on Eden. He hadn't come near me since he'd stepped in Michael's path to protect me.

"Children are blessings," Eden spoke into the microphone. She took in a deep, unnecessary breath and let it out. "I know that because I am your mother."

Her eyes roamed all her creations before her. The weight of her gaze settled into my heart like an anchor that had reached its home port after many years. Then she looked up at the blinking red dot of Tia's camera. I felt the same weight in the air and was certain that every human, every animal, every blade of grass on the surface felt it too.

"You are each my heritage and my reward. You are not servants unto me, you are me. You are from my very light."

From the center of her chest, Eden's light shone even more brightly. It was hard to keep my gaze trained on her. Those watching around the world were likely seeing a white-out. But the smile on her face and feeling in her voice rang true and clear.

"Woe to those who call evil good and good evil, who put darkness for light and light for darkness. There is no such thing as good and evil. There is only life, and it is precious."

A single tear formed in one of her large eyes. At least I think so. It evaporated before it ventured past her eyelid, swallowed back into her essence.

"The only sin on this green Earth is causing death. My message is that you all live. My instruction is that each of you be fruitful and multiply. My prayer is that you learn to trust the light inside you. When you do that you will hear my voice and know that I am the way."

Her light cooled as she spoke. She brought it back into herself. What remained were her abnormal, barely human features. Her overlarge eyes that didn't need to blink. Her tipped ears that curved around the side of her face. Her bald head with the intricate network of raised nodes.

She was the most beautiful thing I'd ever seen in the world. My heart was full at her words, my spirit light.

"Go toward the light," Eden said. "That is all the

instruction you need. Good luck, humanity. I will be watching."

The feed cut and plunged the rectangular box into darkness. We all stared at Eden for a long moment of silence. She looked up from the camera, eyes wide with inquiry.

"How did I do?" Eden asked.

No one had any words. For me, it had been like attending one of those self-help conventions where people come in down on their luck and leave with dreams of taking on the world, their pockets lighter from the confidence game.

But Eden was no con man. She was the real deal. And if humans only heeded her words, this world, their world, would be a better place.

"They'll likely screw it up," said Hestia as she wrapped cables from the makeshift studio set around her arm. "But that's humanity."

Eden rose from her seat in the spotlight and made her way toward me. She reached for my hands. I gave them to her. Her palms were warm, but she didn't show me anything from the past. I could tell her attention now was directed toward the future.

"I want you to keep up your work on the

surface," she said. "Document it all—the good, the bad, and the ugly. Especially the ugly stories."

I inhaled through my nose. So, I would keep my job as record-keeping Ishim. She would probably ask that I return to the core in another few millennia so she could download my memories and judge humanity anew. Once again, not bothering to get her hands dirty.

"I want an accurate accounting when next I come to visit," Eden said.

I gaped. "Come? Up here and visit?"

She nodded. "With your help, I'll be able to see what improvements have been made and what we still need to do to get these children on a sustainable path."

All I could do was nod. We stood there eyeing each other for a moment. Eden's face screwed in uncertainty as she regarded me.

"Would you like a hug?" she asked. "My daughters seem fond of them. Their father indulges them."

"I would," I said. "I'd like that very much, if you don't mind."

Eden opened her arms. I stepped into them. I wrapped my arms around her lithe body. She felt like a fire in the winter, that spot in the center of the bed before the alarm goes off. She may not do hugs a lot, but she was awesome at them and I felt privileged to get one of the rare events.

All too soon she pulled away from me. "Come and visit me every couple of centuries for a chat. We'll make a weekend of it."

"I'd like that," I said.

She turned to go. But then turned back, her brow lifted once again in uncertainty. "Incidentally, what exactly should occur during a mother-daughter weekend?"

"Oh," said Loren, raising her hand. "I can help with that."

Loren looped her arm through Eden's and walked off in the distance. I heard the words chocolate cake, spa treatments, and male strippers. Honestly, yeah, that about covered it.

With Eden in good hands, I came face to face with my father.

"Hi," I said.

Gabriel nodded.

We both stood there awkwardly for a second. He looked at my shoulder. I looked beyond him at the gate.

"Thank you," I tried. "For, you know, saving me from your homicidal brother."

"Michael is not my brother. We did not share a womb." Gabriel pressed his lips together into a thin line. "There is no need to thank me. You are my progeny. We share the same light. Protecting you is akin to protecting myself."

Gabriel frowned as he said the words, as though he wanted to retract some of them. And then his frown screwed into frustration, as though he didn't know what he'd replace the words with.

"I'm proud," I said. "I'm proud to be a part of you. It's an honor to share your light."

Gabriel stood stiff. Then he looked uncomfortable as he tried to loosen his limbs. It was clear he was unused to dealing with emotion of any kind, be it anger, gratitude, or praise.

"I have spoken with Eden. The door will remain open," he said finally. "So that you may visit Vau any time you'd like."

That made my heart sing. To see Vau anytime I wanted. And maybe even nose around a bit in Eden's lab.

"You will need to return with some frequency if you want to avoid the allergy between you and Zayin," Gabriel was saying.

"I'll do that." I paused, biting my lip. Then I just came out with it. If I was going to be visiting, he'd have to get used to more emotions coming his way. "Would it be all right if I stopped by to say hi to you when I come?"

Gabriel nodded slowly. "I would have no objection to that."

I reached out one hand. A hug would be asking too much. For now. But maybe in a couple of decades, who knew? I might give my dad a kiss on the cheek within the next century.

"Thank you, Gabriel."

He nodded stiffly. Then he left to join Eden, who was preparing to take off with the other Elohim parents. They huddled together, not touching. Their skin melted away until they were nothing but light.

We Ishim huddled on the surface watching the light show our parents made for us, like a Fourth of July spectacular. And then they left us behind. But this time when they left us, it was different.

We were no longer aimless, rudderless, or without direction. We each had a purpose now, and that was to steer humanity on their path toward sustainability and salvation.

Yup. We were screwed.

Zane came up behind me and snugly wrapped his arms around me. He shifted until the back of my head was cradled in the spot just under his chin—my spot.

"You're an amazing woman," he said. "You just saved the world."

"And I got to go to Disney World," I snorted.

The park was destroyed. The next Super Bowl winners would not come here for a victory party any time soon. But at least they still would be able to play on the turf known as Earth instead of being expunged in total annihilation.

The bright colors in the sky our parents had left with had changed. The colors muted into something more pink and purple. It was fuchsia.

"Look at that," I said. "It's the color of fuckweasel."

Zane chuckled. "You'd look perfect against that backdrop."

His breath tickled the top of my ear. Then he gasped a hot breath. I thought things were about to get interesting, but he pulled away.

Zane held me out in front of him, staring intently as he positioned me this way and then that way.

"Oh no, you don't," I groaned.

He ignored my protest and tilted my chin, scrutinizing the placement of my cheeks.

"Zane. Not now."

"Hold still, just a moment." He leaned down, and instead of pulling out paper and pencil, he kissed my nose. "I'm not going to paint it. I just want to remember it. Always."

"No need." I held still for him as he pulled away, like I always did. Like I always would. "I'm not going anywhere."

EPILOGUE

"Seriously?" groaned Zane. "You're using charcoal instead of wood?"

Zane looked down as Tres piled charcoal into a grill that looked as though it came out of a top chef's kitchen. The stainless steel was pristine, as though it had never been used. Not a smudge marred the surface. It had four burners, a surface for cutting, and cabinets for storage.

Tres held tongs in one hand and lighter fluid in the other. Across his casual jeans and T-shirt he wore an apron that read *Work Like a Captain, Party Like a Pirate*. The calm sea stretched for miles all around us as we lounged on the deck of his yacht.

"If I use wood," Tres said, "it's not barbecuing."

"Wood gives food a unique taste." Zane grimaced

as he watched his brother spray the dark coals with fluid. "That's too much."

"Wood gives it a unique taste, all right," said Tres, spritzing just a bit more fluid on the coals. "The taste of blood, since the meat will be raw. Wood can't hold its heat."

"You put on more fluid on purpose," Zane complained.

Tres slammed the container of fluid down and held the tongs in front of Zane's face. He snapped the two sides of the metallic teeth together in a menacing fashion. "I've been putting food into fire for longer than you've been alive."

"The age card?" said Zane. "Is that your defense?"

"Respect your elders, kid."

"Not when they're going senile." Zane struck a match and tossed it into the pit. The fire caught in midair before the match even landed. The blaze reached high and both men reared back.

They eyed one another, and seeing neither was singed, they each cracked a grin. Then they turned back, arms crossed over their chests, and admired the flame.

Loren and I watched from our vantage point a short distance away, lounging in bikinis and deck chairs. The two brothers had been like this since we'd left Florida. At each other's throats one hour, clapping each other on the back like the best of friends the next minute, only to try and clobber each other in a competitive streak in the following second.

It was dizzying. It was also heartening. I was pretty sure it was normal too.

Many of my memories were within reach with this flesh still being new. There were some times when I was uncertain if I was watching Zane and Tres in the present or remembering a time in our shared past. Though I was pretty sure I didn't have a lot of memories of us sailing the world together.

Tres's yacht was opulence on steroids, which pretty much described its owner. Unlike when we'd sailed from Istanbul to Athens, there was no crew. We were the only four souls on the boat.

"This is a different boat, isn't it?" I turned to Loren. "From the one we sailed to Greece in."

"Oh yeah." Loren nodded. "The other one is at the bottom of the Bermuda Triangle, which is actually an entrance into the nine realms. The boat was given in tribute to Rán and Aegir."

She spoke nonchalantly. I'd only gotten bits and pieces of her times and trials in the fae realm. Most of it was pretty unbelievable. She'd mentioned mermaids and flower people and the trickster god Loki. She'd also had a new maturity about her, like the trip had changed her. Much like the night of the apocalypse turning out to be humanity's salvation.

Despite Eden's direct satellite television message, many humans doubted the whole spectacle was real. The government still maintained that it was a result of hackers breaking into the Emergency Alert System and was now angling to raise taxes to upgrade cyber defense.

There were a few believers. Pockets of humanity had left their jobs to start communes where they walked around naked and worshiped the light. The light as in any source of light: the sun, the bulbs, the bugs.

The prevailing theory was that it was all a stunt put on by producers at Disney in preparation for their next big-budget film. With such interest, of course producers pounced on the idea. A new film about the apocalypse was currently in production in Hollywood. In fact, one of the producers was none other than a certain Greek God. However, at no fault of Desi's, both the savior and God in the film were rumored to be recast as men because males tested better in those roles than women.

The human mind had such an ability to compartmentalize things into their preferred view of the world. I dreaded my first meeting with Eden on the progress of humanity. But no one could say they hadn't been warned.

The smell of something delicious drew my attention back to the happenings at the grill. Tres was grinning at something Zane had said. Tres's eyes softened when he noticed me staring. His grin spread wider to include me.

My heart was so full in this moment, I worried that some of my feelings might get pushed too far down and forgotten, just like my memories. But that wasn't possible, not any longer.

I'd always believed that every story had an ending. Even one that twisted and wound as the four of ours did. We'd gone forward, reverse, up and down, and even crisscross.

We weren't linear. We were a circle of friends whose connections were inevitable. And there was no end in sight.

These were the three most important people in my life and I would never let them too far or too long out of my life. With that promise latched firmly in my mind, I settled back in my seat.

Tres looked past me at Loren. The affection in

his eyes shifted. Instead of a slow-burning piece of charcoal, the light in his eyes flared like a piece of wood over a flame.

Loren was looking off into the horizon. She'd definitely changed since I'd last seen her. There was a wisdom in her blue eyes, like she'd seen things.

It was like I was seeing her for the first time again. I remembered that buttoned-up woman in a business suit who'd followed me down a flight of stairs back in D.C. She'd lured me on an adventure I hadn't quite been prepared for, and here we were still.

"Did you do something different with your hair?" I said. "It looks like it's shining."

"My hair has been under a lot of scrutiny lately." She twirled a curl around her finger. "These locks almost got me hitched back in Asgard."

"Married? You mentioned something about an engagement. You never mentioned to who?"

Loren's attention shifted to the grill.

"You mentioned Loki and Thor."

She nodded, still eyeing the grill.

"Which one?"

"Thor."

"Thor? The Norse god of thunder proposed to you?"

"Yup." She sighed.

"And you said..." I prompted her, dying to know her answer.

"I didn't." Loren shrugged. "I was too busy trying to figure out a way to save my bestie."

"And now that I'm saved?"

"Nia, you know I'm not the marrying kind."

"No," I said. "I don't know that. You deserve a happily ever after, especially after... He Who Shall Not Be Named."

Loren wrinkled her nose. I was glad to see that mention of her ex-lover, Leonidas Baros, no longer caused her any pain.

"I will need to meet this thunder god, to make sure he's good enough for my best friend. That's what besties do. Check out each other's men."

Loren had been taking a sip of wine, but she choked. She sat the glass down at the deck. "Oh, enough about me. I have a burning question for you."

I waited patiently for her question, but I also marked my place in this conversation because we were so totally coming back to it later. Sooner than later, in fact.

Loren took a deep, serious breath and then came out with it. "What is Zane's last name?"

"He's an artist. He only goes by the one."

"Like Prince or Madonna?"

"Exactly," I said. "Now I have a burning question for you."

"Yes, these are my real boobs."

But I wasn't about to be deterred. "What's going on with you and Tres?"

A flush crept across her cheeks. A sheen of sweat broke out across her brow.

Then Loren straightened her spine. She looked me dead in the eye, her blue eyes filled with a seriousness I had only seen once before in our short lifetime together. She beckoned me with a wave of her fingers, and I came closer into her confidence.

"Do you really want to talk about boys, Dr. Rivers?" she said. "Or do you want to go on an adventure?"

My lips parted wider and wider until I was grinning. This idea had the makings of even more trouble. But I already knew what I was getting into.

"Sure," I said. "I could use an adventure."

ALSO BY INES JOHNSON

Lover of fairytales, folklore, and mythology, Ines Johnson spends her days reimagining the stories of old in a modern world. She writes books where damsels cause the distress, princesses wield swords, and moms save the world.

You can sign up for her mailing list and receive alerts and free reads at http://bit.ly/InesReaders.

The Nia Rivers Adventures

Dragon Bones

Demeter's Tablet

Templar Scrolls

Serpent Mound

Eden's Garden

The Misadventures of Loren

Spear of Destiny

Ring of Gyges

Hammer of God

www.ingramcontent.com/pod-product-compliance
Lightning Source LLC
LaVergne TN
LVHW012035070526
838202LV00056B/5505